The Secret Diary of Misty Brown

Denise Litchmore

Published by Denise Litchmore, 2022.

This is a work of fiction. Similarities to real people, places, or events are entirely coincidental.

THE SECRET DIARY OF MISTY BROWN

First edition. December 18, 2022.

ISBN: 979-8201942861

Written by Denise Litchmore.

Dedication:

To Jordan and Tia, who are my heartbeats

CHAPTER 1:

I SMOKE,
THEREFORE I AM

DEAR DIARY,

I cannot believe that I am 42 and a half years old. The half is important for no other reason other than that it reminds me of Adrian Mole, which tickles me and reminds me of my lost youth!

My motto is: I smoke, and drink, and, therefore, I am ... never knowingly without a cigarette, a glass of Captain Morgan rum and a bag of ready salted crisps.

When Kiki was in labour, and I insisted that we stop on route to hospital, so I could stock up on cigarettes, I realised, with some satisfaction, that I am a true cigarette addict...

I really don't know why she wasted time complaining, or why I had to explain that 'It is going to be a long night for me ... I am going to have to prop you up, Kiki, wipe your fevered brow, stuff things in your mouth so you don't annoy me with your screaming, and try to make sure that the infant exploding forth from your nether regions is not too ugly....being primed to push him back in if he is really very ugly....All this will be impossible without fags....you know how I get without nicotine'. She caved and, of course, we knew she would....what else can little sisters do when faced by the logic espoused by a big sister?

She did add, 'If I have the baby in the Esso petrol station, I will hurt you quite badly'... which seemed fair enough.

Cigarettes and I are a couple ...not one of those sickly sweet couples you see cuddled up with sickening public displays of affection, oh no, no! Cigarettes and I have been together for years; I was barely legal when we met and at the ripe age of sixteen, they seduced me with their smoky aroma and I was theirs forever...forsaking all others for the delights of their smoky haze...We speak sparingly but understand each other perfectly...we are an amazing team.

NAUGHTY BUT NICE

DEAR DIARY,

When I was 10 years old, my world consisted of family, my parents, my siblings, my uncle/ godfather, aunts and cousins. There was a rich family connection between us that didn't need, or want, external interruptions and I basked in being loved, cared for and enjoyed by my family.

I was a precocious child, much given to flights of fancy, strange whims and naughtiness in equal measure, so I was no stranger to the slipper, which was used regularly to try to discipline me. This was to no avail since I remained wonderfully undisciplined, cheeky and intransigent.

I blame my naughtiness on my godfather, who was a wonderful man and smiled indulgently whenever I did something wrong. He nicknamed me 'trouble' with delight and refused to allow my parents to apply the slipper whenever I was naughty in his presence, which was rather frequently, as I was nothing if not consistent in my naughtiness.

I think my descent into wilfulness, oppositional behaviour and defiance began in my childhood, and I have spent an inordinate amount of time in my adulthood enjoying hedonistic pleasures and then trying to recover from them, with varying degrees of success...from sublime childhood, to Fatty McFatty, nicotine addiction and a serious penchant for alcoholic beverages!

DAY ZERO

ON MONDAY, I WOKE UP and went to work as usual, rode the 185 bus as usual, got off at my usual bus stop and alighted, in my usual place, lighting my third cigarette of the day. I thought that this was just a usual Monday and I had no idea of the cataclysmic change about to occur!

People who have never smoked won't understand the utter gloriousness of it. When I hold that lovely, fresh new packet in my hand, peel away the cellophane wrapping, which glints in the light, tip the first slim fella from the packet and marvel at his gorgeousness! I put him to my lips and, with a flick of the lighter, I drag him deep into my mouth, inhaling that lovely acrid smoke and exhaling it in one wonderful plume. Absolutely fantastic! Well, there I was puffing on the little fella, minding my own business, deeply engrossed in Bella magazine, when, out of the blue, my eyes were assaulted by a story about a mum giving up smoking. I wanted no truck with it and prepared to read something else, but my eyes were inextricably drawn back to it, despite the fact that I thought that she was a bit ridiculous to want to give up smoking. I was proud that, in 26 years of smoking, I had never tried to give it up, because as far as I was concerned it was a delightful habit and a great accompaniment to everything!

Anyhoo, there I am reading about this woman who actually had the temerity to listen to her children and, as a result, foolishly give up smoking; I realised that I had an uncomfortable feeling forming in my stomach and idly wondered whether the fish I ate last night was off. The woman in the story said that her children regularly pleaded with her to stop smoking and that she had stopped being able to reassure them that smoking was harmless. Suddenly, I had a vision of my daughter reciting all matter of harmful facts about smoking that she had learnt at school, asking me not to smoke anymore, with me explaining that this was information for ordinary folk and, since I was super mum, I would be absolutely fine. I read on with growing unease, as I was deeply aware of a feeling of foreboding and a shift in the atmosphere. I felt a tide of emotion rising within me. By the end of the article, I was gulping for air, tears were streaming down my face and I was in the grip of a horrible and, powerfully emotional, realisation that smoking was bad! Oh dear Lord! How had that happened? What the hell was I going to do now? A woman passed by and noticed that I was in the grip of a maelstrom. She asked if I was ok and I all but fell on her, as she made the mistake of trying to pat my shoulder. I gripped her arms in a state of high agitation and wailed, 'Oh my god! I have to give up smoking'. She eyed me in alarm and backed away, grimacing. I let her go and slumped on a convenient wall, deciding that being late to work when such catastrophe had befallen me was absolutely justifiable and, if my manager disagreed, I would have to slap him really hard until he came to his senses.

Denial had left the building. Suddenly, I saw myself through the eyes of my friends, family and children. If my friends dared to say no when I wanted to sully their homes with my smoking, I refused to visit until they gave in. Such was my awesomeness that they usually didn't put up much of a fight. When my dad refused to allow myself and my siblings to smoke during our visits, I tapped into his parental guilt, gave him a hard stare, elongated the word 'daddy' and he caved.

When my children, my darling angelic cherubs....all right they weren't always cherubic and sometimes I did wonder if they were the spawn of Beelzebub, but they are mine and whilst I did contemplate selling them for a pound to random strangers on occasion, I was really rather fond of them....when they asked me to stop smoking, I would pat them on the head and say, 'don't be silly, now run along and play'. But the scales had fallen from my eyes; I had realised the extent of my folly and I had decided, at the ripe old age of 42, to stop smoking.

—— ⬤ ——

I HAVE SEEN THE LIGHT

—— ⬤ ——

I WOKE IN EXCITEMENT today because I've seen the light and have had a revelation. If I stop smoking, I can buy more shoes!! Of course I'll be healthier, have more time to spend with the children, won't die of a smoke-related disease, but I will also... and this is so much more important, be able to afford those shoes I coveted in the local shop last week. They called to me from the depths of the store – all new and shiny – and begged me to save them from their confinement to walk proudly down the street, whilst everyone admired their beauty. But alas, although they had beseeched me, cried and finally turned ugly and hurled insults, I had to walk away. But now I will return to them and there will be much kissing and hugging. I know I will have to apologise, but this is only fair. I know I will have to promise to look after them and forsake all others, and I will, of course, but I will be lying because I now have the extra cash to purchase even more shoes and ... boots ... and bags and glory, glory ... new joys ... lipsticks!!!

I haven't taken this decision lightly. I've considered this long and hard, and have realised I would have to make many sacrifices; no more shooing the children away so I can smoke long into the night. Now, I will, doubtless, have to spend time with them. No more only eating half of my dinner so I can have a quick fag; no more standing outside in the cold with my clique of 'friends', who were banished to the pavement by evil non-smokers. No more considering whether I can cope with that long flight to Thailand and opting for a week in Spain instead. No more buying shares in Oust and Febreze just to get the marvellous smell of smoke out of my curtains. No more jumping up from a warm bed and legging it to the corner shop on a Sunday morning because I need my morning fag... and no more fag breath! Oh yes, sacrifices will be made aplenty, but I think – on balance I'm up for it.

WHITE STICK

D-DAY IS THE 21ST FEBRUARY. I need a long lead-in time to give myself time to enjoy the last 200 or so cigarettes. I plan a long day of shopping and Lorena has promised to take me out to do something marvellous on the 20th, so that my last day as a smoker is memorable. As we have been friends for over 20 years, I trust her not to lead me into temptation ... well not much. I recall a memorable Miami trip when we were in our 20s. We led each other into very bad, very naughty temptation; but we are very old now and, therefore, fully capable of exercising restraint ... well – sometimes.

I am very over excited and have got the patches in readiness for a full-frontal assault. I know that I am weak willed (well, sometimes) and that cigarettes and I have been friends for many years, so I fully expect tears, recriminations, huffs and possibly violence from my old friend. But, I will be armed and ready to do battle. The GP has provided me with patches and whilst I am viewing these with some suspicion, I'm fully prepared to accept that these little squares are up to the challenge against my little white sticks. If they fail, I accept no responsibility; white stick is a formidable opponent and I anticipate a bloody battle. I will, obviously, check in on patch and stick from time to time to see how they are faring. I'll run my eye over them for obvious signs of attack, possibly offer mouth to mouth to patch when necessary; but ... I will have no truck with white stick, as I will be on my way to the shoe shop.

I have tried to motivate my sisters to join me in casting out white stick from their lives, but I have cautioned them to think carefully, to remember they will miss him and will need to think about things to replace him in their lives. If, like me they have strong feelings for shoes (lipsticks, bags, etc) they may be fine. If however, they have no other outlets for their devotion, I strongly urge caution since they may become devoted to something nasty, like bad men, drink, daytime telly or – horror of horror – food. Ultimately, if they succumb to the latter temptation, this will no doubt end badly and will lead to them becoming rather round, their husbands chucking them out, people pointing at them in the street, children spurning them at the school gates and not being able to look at themselves in the mirror. Thereby, ending in costly therapy (no money for shoes) and a withdrawal from the world.

So, they will need to think hard, if they are looking to change their life – taking up golf or ballroom dancing may be better options – but if they insist on following me into the great unknown, they must be prepared for the uphill struggle, the tears, the sacrifices, the yearning, the desire ... the gut wrenching all-consuming need for a fag.

BERT

I HAD MY LAST CEREMONIAL cigarette at midnight on Friday 20th February. Then I had another six, because I just didn't want to say goodbye. I named my final cigarette Bert and we had a little chat about the good times and how he's always been a dependable sort of chap, gotten me out of a few scrapes in my time, been a good friend in times of need and, all right, yes, he may have tried to kill me once or twice, made my breath smell and made me a tad anti-social, because he often wanted me all to himself. But when the chips were down, Bert was my mate.

THE GREAT UNKNOWN

SATURDAY 21ST FEBRUARY dawned bright and early and I rolled over and reached for my cigarettes on my bedside table, but they weren't there! Immediately, panic engulfed me and I started thinking wildly about cigarette thieves. One of these dastardly fellas had obviously snuck into my house last night, crept into my bedroom and taken my precious cigarettes for their all-consuming smoking pleasure. Slightly wild about the eyes, I cast furtive glances into the recesses of the room and clutched the bedcovers around me lest they were still in the house and intent on further marauding in their hunt for more contraband. The sleep haze lifted before I called the police ... then I remembered that I no longer smoke.

I felt excitement rising, as I was now ready to go forward into the great unknown, the world of non-smokers. I slapped on a patch, being careful to put it very near my throat, so the nicotine wouldn't have far to travel. I waited for the rush, but it didn't happen, so I toyed with the idea of slapping on another one, perhaps in my mouth, just to help the first one along. But I resisted the urge and went about my morning as usual ... but it's not usual, it's flipping unusual, because nothing is the same anymore.

After breakfast, I looked for my cigarettes, always a wonderful after-breakfast treat, and remembered that I don't smoke. My lip started to tremble and I felt a bit sorry for myself, so I dropped the children off at school tearfully hugging them and promising that mummy wasn't dying ... she had just stopped smoking.

I contemplated a life without cigarettes stretching to infinity and then it hit me ... I remembered; I have marvellous things to look forward to as I am going shopping at the weekend to buy shoes!!

I went into my office, closed the door and slumped at my desk. All this not smoking lark was exhausting! I tried to concentrate on looking through case notes and getting on with my day, but I was starting to feel something unpleasant rising and unfurling from the pit of my stomach. One of my lovely staff, Rosalyn, knocked on my door and asked if she could talk to me about one of her cases. Usually, I love being a team manager in customer services, but, today, I had problems of my own! Rosalyn wandered in, sat down and prepared to discuss a knotty problem. Usually, I'm all ears, but, for some reason, the shape of Rosalyn's head was annoying me. I looked at her balefully and asked whether she absolutely needed to talk to me now and she insisted that she did. In fairness to me, I had given her an out, which she had refused to take, so what followed next was entirely her fault. She began talking and I started frantically sniffing the air. Was that smoke I could smell emanating from about her person? I heard not a word she said, as I was trying to inhale the smoke from her clothes. Finally, I interrupted her flow and asked if she had been smoking. She answered in the affirmative and a beatific smile settled on my countenance. 'Rosalyn', I asked silkily, 'I seem to have forgotten my cigarettes, so can I have one of yours?' She eyed me warily because I am her manager after all, and bravely said 'no'. She went on to tell me that I had emailed the entire staff team yesterday and told them that if I asked them for a cigarette, they were to refuse me. 'Don't be ridiculous!' I roared, 'Of course I didn't mean that ... the balance of my mind had clearly been altered!' She backed out of the office, trying not to run, and called for re-enforcements as she went. My manager, Stewart, came into the office and sat tentatively in a chair. 'Are you ok, Misty...?' he asked. '...Only Rosalyn seems a little upset and I wondered if all is well?' I eyed him with distaste and explained that my employee had refused to give me a cigarette and, therefore, I was contemplating sacking her for gross misconduct. Stewart didn't appear to understand the precarious nature of his predicament and proceeded to tell me that I couldn't sack her and that refusing your manager a cigarette was not grounds for sacking. I felt a clawing in my gut ... I felt panicky and out of control and I warned him that 'if someone didn't bring me a cigarette, and pronto, they would rue the day!' Stewart wondered 'whether it might be a good idea for me to take the day off, or work from home,' (and visit my GP or an exorcist as my head appeared to swinging round at a 180 degree angle ... on close inspection, I also appeared to be foaming at the mouth). I agreed that this was probably for the best and left for the day.

CHAPTER 2:
MOURNING

I HAVE DESCENDED INTO mourning, as I have now become one of those non-smoking folk I used to sneer and jeer at, as being uninteresting, risk averse and as boring as a boring thing, vanilla ... ish! Lacking in taste and flipping boring!

I have always lived my life on the edge ...drinking, smoking, eating delicious sugary and fatty foods. And now one of my favourite friends was gone.

Bert had died ... you know the fella, white body with a brown head, three inches tall and full of smoky flavour! Bert and I had traversed the highways of life together. He was waiting patiently for me until I gave birth, comforted me when my marriage broke down, offered a lovely activity when I was bored and was just my constant companion, loyal to a fault. But now he was gone, never to return and I was so bereft without his comforting presence.

TRIUMPHANT SHOPPING

I COLLECTED MY SMALL girl from her aunties, basking in the fact that I hadn't had a fag in ... ooh, three hours. I met my niece and we all had a marvellous time shopping. Unfortunately, my daughter started complaining about her feet, so I told her to 'stop being a baby and put your back into it', threatened to tell her friends that she 'couldn't shop for toffee', and likened her to 'a man!!' but she still insisted we head back home after a measly eight hours shopping. Weak, but I blame myself. I've obviously not shown her how it's done. But practice makes perfect and we're off out again in a fortnight.

I came home triumphant with a pair of shoes ...oh yeah ... and boots, and hmm yes, managed to get a little make-up too. The kids had bags, so I guess I must have bought them something, but I can't really recall since I was busy making the acquaintance of my new shoes.

After a hard day's shopping, I thought I would treat myself to a glass of wine. Unfortunately, the sad truth is that it doesn't taste the same without a fag. It's almost redundant, which, I guess, is good news for my liver, although I do see it as my duty to push through. I will try my best not to lessen my wine and rum intake, otherwise the shock to my body at losing two such good friends at once might prove fatal.

SMOKE, KILL

AFTER SATURDAY'S SUCCESS, I thought Sunday would be a breeze. I was wrong. The whole day I had two thoughts. Smoke ...Kill. That's it. Smoke – Kill. This wasn't me considering my options, this was my mission statement. Kiki came to visit, and when she started to smoke, I'm afraid that I behaved badly, considered killing her (only briefly), and wanted to roar, 'stop flipping smoking around me!!' But I was trying to hang onto my dignity, so I began annoying her instead. I think she had planned to stay for dinner, but clearly bile and vitriol with her meal was no longer an appetising option, so she grabbed her bag and fled. I eyed my children speculatively. They eyed me back nervously, and backed away with unseemly haste to the relative safety of their rooms. My son went one further and left the house altogether, with hasty instructions to my daughter to 'stay in your room – don't come out for anything – I'll bring you food and water when I get back'.

So I spent the rest of the evening banging seven bells out of the pots and pans, whilst I cooked what was probably going to be an inedible meal, since I spent most of the time swearing at the meat, casting aspersions on the character of the potatoes, and telling the veg that their parentage was questionable at best...

EATING MACHINE

I TRIED TO CRAM THE entire contents of the kitchen cupboards and the fridge into my mouth. I don't really eat ice-cream, so I had three Cornettos, three family packets of cheesy Wotsits, my dinner, my daughter's leftover dinner, my son's potato (which he was attempting to eat until I grabbed it off his fork) a bar of chocolate, a slice of angel cake (well, half the cake), two apples, three satsumas and an entire bunch of grapes. My daughter told me that, 'tomorrow is another day' and 'I shouldn't have eaten all the grapes', since she was planning to have a few grapes for her packed lunch tomorrow. I thought this was very brave of her, considering that my eyes had glazed over, my shoulders were hunched up to my ears and I was engaged in shouting obscenities at the TV. I quietly suggested that, perhaps, she should consider having a KitKat for lunch instead, or move out and buy her own grapes. Not smoking is having a marvellous impact on my temperament, my appetite and my parenting skills.

NOTHING TO LOOK FORWARD TO

NOW, DEAR DIARY,

I'm going to share something with you, but don't laugh at me. Well, all right, you can ... but only for a minute.

I feel like I have nothing to look forward to. Food seems less interesting. Wine seems less tasty cos I'm no longer sipping and taking in marvellous lungs full of nicotine at the same time. Watching telly seems boring, because I can't quickly light a fag when it's coming to the exciting bit of the show. Talking on the phone is less appealing, cos I can't say, 'hang on, hang on, hold the thought....no don't tell me yet, just let me light a fag, cos I think I'm gonna need it!!'.

You see what I neglected to consider before embarking on this journey was that 'white stick' has been with me for life's big and small events for 26 years. He's been my shoulder to lean on, cry and laugh with and now he's gone. He left me in my hour of need, abandoned me to my own devices,

the heartless little **@@!!..........

'CIGARETTES NOT SMOKED' TIME

I AM NOW ON DAY 12. The urge to kill has left me, but I am aware that she is lurking just behind the patch, waiting to jump out and maim, if someone, anyone at all, annoys me. I am still counting the hours in 'cigarettes not smoked time', but I've managed to resist the urge to run out and beg 'white stick' to take me back and be mine forever.

Today is better than yesterday, so, hopefully, tomorrow will be better than today. Unfortunately, I can't go shopping every day and the only thing standing between me and a cigarette is me. It's a scary thought, but perhaps I have more willpower

than I realised.

The good news is the patches do work cos they take the edge off, but the urge to bawl (loudly), moan and tear my clothes is never very far away. So, I am liable to be found crying uncontrollably in the street, grabbing at strangers and trying to tell them what 'patch is doing' to my relationship with 'white stick' in the throes of trying to kick the habit.

BERT'S IN A HUFF

I WENT TO THE SHOP today and Bert was there! We greeted each other like long-lost lovers. We exchanged pleasantries and Bert said he was feeling 'fair to middling' and I said it had been hell without him and I couldn't bear it. Bert suggested that it was easily remedied and I just needed to buy him. It would be the work of an instant and we could be cosied up in a trice. Tearfully, I told him no and said we could no longer be. He glared at me, called me 'a fair-weather friend', intimated that I had poor hygiene, as I always smelt of smoke and said he hadn't liked me anyway, whereupon he turned away in a huff.

IN MY DEFENCE

DEAR LORD, SAVE ME from this all-consuming, gut-wrenching need for a fag! Jacqueline came over for a visit and told me that Kiki had explained that I was a bit overwrought and, as my big sister, she thought she should check on me and see if I had cracked yet. In the interests of science, she explained that it was her duty to smoke around me so that we could determine the extent of my willpower. She proceeded to smoke herself silly, with me waving my arm expansively and saying, 'No, don't be silly, you don't have to go outside, you enjoy your fag'. Meanwhile, I was hypnotised, watching her hand-to-mouth action, but congratulating myself and feeling smug that I wasn't trying to wrestle her to floor, grab the fag, stuff it in my face and smoke the whole thing in one drag.....I was a veritable saint, demonstrating marvellous restraint. Unfortunately, the visit ended badly and I have apologised profusely for punching her repeatedly in the face, but ... in my defence, she wouldn't let go of the cigarette.

DARKENED DOORWAYS

YOU WOULD THINK THAT, after 15 days of not smoking, I would feel like one of those 'non-smoker folk'. But I don't. I still long to be affiliated with those marvellous people, spending their time in darkened doorways, shunned by normal folk. Relegated to standing outside houses, shops and places of business to conduct their clandestine meetings with other smokers. Shoulders hunched against the wind ... cupping their palms around their lighter ... and drawing in that first delicious blast of nicotine.

I eye up my colleagues' fags with ill-concealed desire and consider the implications of 'just one fag'. I must confess that, on a dark winter's night, some six days ago, I succumbed to temptation and Bert had his way with me once more. We only did it once (all right twice), but I must confess that I lay awake thinking about him and longed for more....

I have decided that it is best if I just stay in bed and withdraw from the world. I am so beyond bored, lonely and irritable as hell, because without my constant white-stick companion, I no longer have any reason for living. Everything is flat and white with no shades of grey and I really don't think I'm long for this world, so I will just drink more merlot, throw some Captain Morgan into the mix (he's always up for it), eat more ready-salted crisps and contemplate the nothingness.

DRYCLEANERS DAY

I WENT TO THE DRYCLEANERS today. I love drycleaners. They smell so fabulously fresh and I love watching all the clothes tumbling round the machine. I went in, greeted the lady behind the counter and gave her my ticket. I had missed this particular jacket, particularly as it was black, had marvellous slimming properties and was an old favourite. After a rummage in the back, she came back to the counter with a fretful expression and explained that she couldn't find my item. In fairness to her, she was gone for ages and had probably had a good look before coming back to me. But, in fairness to me, I hadn't smoked for 16 days, so I think I win! I rested my arm on the counter, took a deep breath and told her that I was fairly sure that her mother didn't know who her father was! I asked whether she understood that I hadn't smoked in 16 days and that all that was standing between her, me and a really good thump was the fact that I was sure that if I gave her three minutes she would find my jacket. She found it in two minutes and all was right with the world. I apologised and, as an ex-smoker, she assured me that she completely understood.

PATCH! PATCH! WHERE ARE YOU?

---◦◦◦---

TODAY I LOST MY PATCHES! I have no idea where I put the stupid things...sorry not stupid, essential, lifesaving things. Forget I said that. I apologise profusely to the patch fairies.

I rang the surgery made an appointment to attend, as I explained to the receptionist that it was a dire emergency and hotfooted it to the surgery to replace my patches. I was told that there would be a bit of a wait, as doctor was running behind and twitchiness began to assail me. Luckily, I didn't have to wait too long and had my prescription clutched in my sweaty hands in a trice. The line at the chemists was long and the woman in front insisted on regaling the entire shop with tales of her lumbago. Steam was pouring out of my ears and I had to restrain myself from shouting, 'We don't care about your flipping lumbago lady! Can't you see I'm a woman on a mission??' Finally, I reached the counter, handed over my prescription and waited impatiently. By this point, I had been some hours without nicotine and was feeling a tad explosive. The counter lady asked me to take a seat and explained that they may not have my particular strength of patch in stock. I waited even more impatiently but couldn't sit still. I perused the stock of birthday cards, played with the condom selection and chose a couple of lollipops. The counter lady returned and informed me that my patch was not in stock, but gaily informed me that it would be in stock tomorrow. Through gritted teeth I asked her, 'What, pray tell, should I do until tomorrow?' She suggested I use what I have at home. I am very sorry for what happened next, but I was at breaking point and it had been seventeen days since I had had a cigarette. I restacked the shelves, paid for the smashed condom case to be replaced, apologised for telling her that her children were the ugliest children I had ever seen, and promised that I would never return to her shop.

FULL BODIED WITH OAK TONES

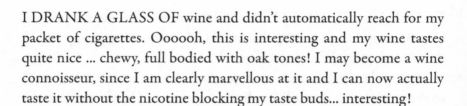

I DRANK A GLASS OF wine and didn't automatically reach for my packet of cigarettes. Oooooh, this is interesting and my wine tastes quite nice ... chewy, full bodied with oak tones! I may become a wine connoisseur, since I am clearly marvellous at it and I can now actually taste it without the nicotine blocking my taste buds... interesting!

CHAPTER 3: DATING – ALL MANNER OF INTERESTING FOLK

OVER THE WEEKEND, I had a discussion on relationships with the family. I love that we're a noisy bunch, always have an opinion on everything and always think we're right. We are equal opportunities opinionated, though, so we don't discriminate. Everyone is allowed to have a view and then everyone has a chance to say, 'Shut up! Your view is rubbish! Never heard such crap'. Anyway, lively banter ensued and everyone got all fired up about what makes a relationship work and how to ensure your partner continues to adore you for the rest of your life. Apparently, always keeping your husband's belly full is the key to success; 'biggin him up' and making him feel that he can achieve anything was ranked highly; and demonstrating that you adore him all day every day is another winner, which apparently leads him to adore *you* all day, every day. We think we hit on the 'formula' a couple of times, but we were wrong. At the end of the night, we wiped up the blood, agreed to disagree with each other and formed our own opinions.

So, today I made my list of requirements... those who won't ever make the grade – fools without un-descended testicles, mummy's boys and 'player, players' – need not apply for the position of 'He, who will be King'. I was told by some women that the type of man I wanted is now an endangered species and only to be found hanging off the arm of some other woman (their wife, girlfriend). Naturally, I ignored these women since I was sure that I had sighted some of these unattached specimens on my travels.

To begin the search for one's King, one must be clear about the Queenly attributes one possesses, so I considered my attributes: womanly figure (slightly round in the thigh and tummy area), magnificent chest, good sense of humour, ability to drink sixteen men under the table, good job, non-smoker (only recently and the jury is still out), fiercely loyal, good cook. All that and a bag of chips – the Personal Ad writes itself!!

Then, I considered those attributes I wanted in a potential 'life partner' – dark, slim, tall, reasonably attractive (doesn't have a face that would scare small children), job (any job, anything at all), nice eyes, enjoys emptying bins and doing the washing up, would become deeply distressed if I attempted to carry the shopping bags, and enjoys whipping up a four course meal when I've had a hard day at work. Whenever I cook, he'd exclaim, 'Oh darling, that's wonderful!' ... and, above all, he will consider me his Queen.

So I signed up – again – to a dating site. I've never had as much fun in my nightie with my rollers in! Where else can you meet 10 potential mates in one night, who may reside in Birmingham or Timbuktu? I wrote I am a non-smoking, yummy mummy of two, etc, etc. It looked funny writing non-smoker, but I felt terribly grown up and a bit smug. I don't smoke ya know! Huge powers of willpower me ... marvellous self-restraint and pretty damn fabulous. Single men look out! I'm the full package – voluptuous (not fat), non-smoker, home maker, sexy bad, so all that and a bag of chips! Internet dating is lovely. Men ogle your picture, send you winks and messages, and you meet all manner of weird and interesting folk.

Yesterday, George sent me a message and told me that I was beautiful and sexy and that he was mad keen to make my acquaintance.

Unfortunately, I declined since George is in the military, lives in another country and is only 24! I know I am truly delightful, but I could smell the baby powder from here! No I do not want to engage in flirtatious banter with a man young enough to be my son. George was inconsolable, so I blocked him to save him any further upset.

I received a message from Roderick today. He had actually read my profile and hadn't just spent time ogling my legs. He had his own teeth, bald – so no receding hairline, beautiful brown skin, fit and attractive. It was one line, but I liked his picture and agreed to exchange more pleasantries via instant messaging. He looks promising and I may allow him a first date.

LIFE, OR SOMETHING LIKE IT

I HAVE DECIDED TO EMBRACE life and ignore everything that does not please me. Much like Marie Antoinette, if my children demand their dinner, I will announce, 'Let them eat cake (or KFC)'. If my boss objects to my leaving early, I will give him a 'hard stare' like Paddington bear – eye him with disdain and flounce from the building. I will continue to pay my mortgage, as homelessness would not suit me, but if the urge arises I will, on occasion, purchase shoes in preference to paying the gas bill. I will no longer confine myself to rigid boundaries about dress – my legs and chest will be on show for all to admire, I will no longer be confined to dating within my age group (well, I guess I wasn't anyway) and I will do what I want, when I want.

Why am I acting in this rebellious fashion? Well, because it comes naturally to me ... but also because I am 42 years old!! I am still struck by the fact that 42 doesn't suit me, I am really much more like a 28 year old, so I've decided that, whilst I will always admit to being 42, I will, henceforth, behave like a 28 year old, as its much more fun.

And...I NO LONGER SMOKE! What the hell do people do with their time?

I have counted my blessings and they are legion. I have marvellous and biddable children, who generally give me much joy; I have a wonderful family, who support me, even when I don't know that I need support. I have amazing friends, who don't care if I don't call them from week to week and will always drop everything if they know I need them. In short, I am incredibly blessed and finally get that I have spent far too much of my very valuable time dwelling on the negative aspects of my life and not rejoicing in the fact that I am alive and doing very well, thank you very much. So, I shall throw caution to the wind, dwell no more on my sagging belly, and swelling cheeks and begin to embrace life.

TAKE WHAT YOU WANT

MY FRIEND MICHAEL HAS urged me to take what I want. I have tried to explain to him that I generally do, but he is not having it and insists that, if I want a particular man, I should just reach out and pluck him! I had a discussion with friends recently where we argued the merits of the direct approach as opposed to the more common coy approach, usually employed by females (well, yes me) when they sight a desirable male. They tried to pretend they didn't know what I was talking about, so I refreshed their memories. You see him ... you glance at him from under your lashes, perhaps you breathe a little harder (better to enhance the chest), look directly at him and make eye contact, then look away, allowing a small smile to play around the lips.

This latter technique allows room to state your interest, but does not require us to jump up and down waving the train into the station with much blowing of whistles and energetic arm thrusts. It preserves our dignity and air of mystique and allows the man the opportunity to chase, because this is what they enjoy and who are we to deny them their enjoyment? Anyway, what's the alternative? We bowl up to them in the street, cock an interested eyebrow and explain that we are seeking a 'lover', life partner or in-betweeny and ask, 'How about it?'

GROWING OLD DISGRACEFULLY

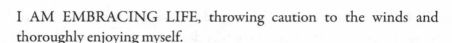

I AM EMBRACING LIFE, throwing caution to the winds and thoroughly enjoying myself.

I met a man on a bus, engaged him in conversation, inveigled him to join me for a drink and then discarded him, (well sort of) because, unfortunately, I discovered that he was only 26. I know I decided not to really consider age, but I thought that if I brought him home, my son might become confused and think that I had brought home a play mate for him. I have begun my descent into growing old very disgracefully.

MR NICE

ANYWAY, I MET MR NICE online and he was a really good bloke, so it's not all serial killers and player, players. I'm as cynical and hard bitten as they come underneath ....well sort of, actually, I'm too optimistic and see sunshine and rainbows everywhere! But online dating is a tool and I use it well, even if I say so myself. I'm a huge romantic and it gives me a little thrill to know that I can talk to people in Manchester, Birmingham and America from the comfort of my own armchair.

Anyway...seriously... how else would I have gotten to meet them – I'm very rarely in America and never in Manchester!!

Let's face it – whilst I may have been pretending not to look, I was, in fact, looking for HIM all along. At the bus stop, at the cinema, and in my purse, in case he'd fallen in with my small change....

Wondering idly whether the man who flashed me at the taxi rank had something meaningful to say and didn't just want me to look at his bits.

DATING – THE RULES

THE 'RULES' ARE NOT for the faint hearted. You must first have abandoned all hope (or be nursing a smidgen in the corner of your heart, but be ready to stamp on it); you must also have been on the 'dating scene' for a while, be prepared to listen to two women talk about the recipe for finding and holding onto that wonderful prize – the esteemed Mr Good Guy!! But just say you're ready – you think, 'aww heck I've tried every other way; so, let's give it a whirl, I think it's worth a read'.

The 'Rules' state that you must be a 'creature like no other'. Now that sounds stupid, right? But it ain't. All it means is that you must value yourself and only consort with men who realise your value. So simple but sooo right.

How many times have we allowed men to 'court' us, just because. We might have thought they were ok – not great, but ok – but did they consider that we were a 'creature like no other', or did they chew their gum thoughtfully and grunt 'yeah, she's alright?' I am now a strict devotee of the rules, not least because, deep down, I know that, whilst I've always valued myself, I haven't always set the right standards and have allowed men to treat me as 'normal', 'all right in a pinch' and 'ok for a laugh'. I have had the true love scenario, too, but, perhaps, because I didn't present like 'a creature like no other', the relationships failed. Who knows? Anyway, when I was in my 20s I knew my value and insisted that people treated me with respect and never settled for less, but I forgot that if you start to feel less than, you present yourself like this. It leaks from you and you begin to settle for less. Less warmth, less love, less respect, less care and devotion and the results ain't pretty.

The 'Rules' say that men should pursue you and if you don't let them, you're taking away their pleasure and joy in life. So you don't call them, they call you. You don't pay, they do. You don't tell them your life story (this ain't a counselling session). You let them know that getting to know you takes time and if they ain't got the time then you say 'NEXT!!!' All this whilst being as subtle as hell. You don't say 'if you don't call me by Wednesday for a Saturday night date, we ain't going, cos I think you're taking me for granted and don't have to plan to see me'. When he calls on Thursday, you just say 'gosh, that would have been fun but I have plans'. Keep making your own plans and he'll get the message that he just needs to call you earlier in the week if he doesn't want you to be tied up with something/someone else!! You don't say 'You don't call/see me enough'... just watch the behaviour. If he doesn't, then make sure you are rarely available and if he comes forward, then great. If he doesn't, you say ... NEXT!! It's so simple.

The 'Rules' urge us to resist our 'urges' and delay intimacy. Well, okay, it's certainly a novel idea anyway!! I asked my friend Maxwell what he thought, since he has never attempted to sleep with me and is, therefore, a marvellous man friend and he told me, 'Yeah, I really wanna work for it. I love it if a woman wants to take it slow, even if, at the same time as I'm looking into her eyes, I'm thinking about how to undo her bra strap and the quickest route to her bed'. 'Yeah, if I hit IT I'm happy, but I'm not really taking her seriously, because I can't help thinking that if I hit IT that quickly, then anybody can'. I was horrified as I'm a 21st-century gal, in charge of my body, my pay cheque and men know that I have needs!

Hmmmm, it seems that some men are keen to return to a simpler time when women wore chastity belts! They want to feel as if you saved yourself for them, that you slept with them because you cared about THEM, not because you had an itch!! If you let them scratch that itch real quick then they think that anyone could have done it for you! Damn! Some men are hard work and whilst I do want a man, I do need one that's a little more of a feminist sympathiser....

CHAPTER 4: A CREATURE LIKE NO OTHER

After reading the 'Rules' I started to think about them. I mean, *really* think. First of all it felt like game playing, or playing hard to get and I thought I'm too honest for that ... I can't do it. Then I thought about past relationships. Those really annoying men who pursued me, even though I told them that they had bad breath, smelt like a cess pit and bored me to death!! They kept ringing, begging to take me out, laying siege at my door. I wasn't playing or treating them mean to keep them keen, I just plain hated them! But they considered that, because I was so unattainable, I must be pretty special and tried their damnedest to get with me. Well the Rules state that you must be 'a creature like no other' and, first, you need to believe it and then act like it.

The 'Rules' are really clear. What I particularly love about them is the idea that if a man doesn't recognise your value, pursue you, want to be around you, then you just say 'Next!!' You don't waste your time, or his, and you move on.

I LOVE it. If he ain't feeling you, just dust yourself down and say, he's just not that into me, so I'll move on!! How liberating is that?!

SATURDAY NIGHT FEVER

I WENT OUT ON SATURDAY night – as you do – and looked forward to a night of drinking, dancing and flirting. By 2am, there were 15 men in the club and 84 women. I began to feel the first stirrings of unease at being surrounded by so many females vying for the attention of the few males, amongst whom, pickings were slim. I mean, if one of these guys sat next to you on the bus, you would move onto another deck if possible or consider walking the eight-mile journey home. But there we were, breaking out the dance moves, laughing and smiling for no good reason, except to look animated and flick back hair with wild abandon. I observed one female clocking a male, doing the shimmy and edging her friend out of the way so that she would be next to him and in his eye line.

We don't mean to act this way, we just feel a strange urge compelling us to snag one of these hapless and, frankly, only passably attractive males. Why? Because we've gone to a lot of flipping trouble. We've been to the hairdressers, agonised over the hip-slimming properties of the little black dress, had our nails done and danced around the bedroom while we got ready to help us get in the mood. We weren't going out with our partners (if we had one), so our mission was obviously to attract a male, or two, just to keep our options open. Yes, okay, we were going to hear the revival and rare groove music, but the point of revival music is to get into a clinch with a stranger (new boyfriend in the making) and dance until you rub off the wallpaper, just like in the good ole days.

The DJ was 'hilarious' and, on at least two occasions, I did consider stuffing my foot in his mouth, since, at regular intervals, he reminded us that there were no men there and then went off into peals of laughter, the stupid, ???@@@!!".

I went with Tanika, who loves to dance. I'm ashamed to say that I added up the number of times she was asked to dance and compared them to my own lamentable tally.....zero. I intercepted one or two hot looks in my direction and did my best to look approachable and up for a dance but, unfortunately, on this occasion, I failed dismally. I was chatted up you understand and I did my best not to yawn or shout, 'How dare you talk to me!?' at the wallies that did engage me in conversation, but, unfortunately, a good night was not had by all. This annoyed me something rotten, because you see, I always ... ALWAYS have a good time! I normally thoroughly enjoy the music, fling my legs about with wild abandon and, usually, and this is very important, usually....I pull......and this kinda rounds off the evening for me. Very shallow, I know, but there you have it. I generally view going out raving as a treat, much as you would a huge chocolate box. Sometimes I know I'm gonna get a hard centre or a creamy caramel, but, ultimately, I'm gonna get me some chocolate and okay, I may feel sick and decide that I am never eating chocolate again, but it's just so yummy I always have just one more.

I soooooo miss smoking and now it appears to be hindering me in getting my dancing groove on!

I SMELL LOVELY

MY DAUGHTER GOT INTO bed with me for a snuggle and said, 'Mummy, you smell lovely... I can't smell cigarettes'. Instead of berating her for her impudence, I found myself laughing and entered enthusiastically into a game of tickle.

SIMPLE THINGS

ON SATURDAY, I DECIDED that since I could no longer go out to play with Bert, I would enjoy spending time with me ... I mean, I do like me. If I had to choose to spend time on a desert island, I would certainly choose to be with me. In the absence of anyone else who enjoys me, then I would certainly rise to the challenge and thoroughly enjoy myself!!!

I waved to my children, who were getting the hell out of my house for the weekend, slammed the door, set the bath and poured myself a glass of wine. Wine tastes marvellous in the bath and I felt mellowed out when I alighted from my bubble bath. I cooked the chicken breasts, stroking them lovingly and telling them how much I was going to enjoy consuming them, and then stuffed them into bagels with lashings of mayonnaise.

I scrolled down my Sky planner and found it ... Independence Day ... with my man, Will Smith. Don't you just love Willy? He's kinda goofy and cute, so you wanna hug him, but then he's got these huge biceps and great skin that make you feel that you may wanna roll around in him a little bit! Maybe get a bit down and dirty ....

Anyhoo, there I am, freshly laundered, plate of chicken and mayo on my left, a bottle of Captain Morgan rum to my right... bliss ...

Will showed me a wonderful time, the chicken enjoyed me eating it, and the Captain was delighted with me.

After the film, I turned my sights to Whitney Houston, switched on the video machine and danced round the living room trying out my dance steps and crooning along. My voice really has got crappy as I've gotten older, but I didn't let that stop me.....

Simple things, simple pleasures and I thoroughly enjoyed my time with me!

QUALITY TIME WITH MY BABIES

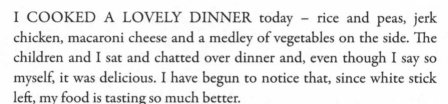

I COOKED A LOVELY DINNER today – rice and peas, jerk chicken, macaroni cheese and a medley of vegetables on the side. The children and I sat and chatted over dinner and, even though I say so myself, it was delicious. I have begun to notice that, since white stick left, my food is tasting so much better.

We lingered over pudding and chatted about this and that, and then my son said, 'Mum this is so nice'. He explained that, normally, I would get up immediately after dinner and go to the kitchen for a cigarette.

I have always found that spending time with one's children can be remarkably overrated, particularly when they are small and sticky, but today was a delightful exception and a reminder that, without white stick's horrible influence, I was really rather a wonderfully attentive mummy!

BEING A MUMMY

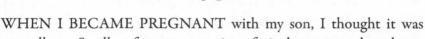

WHEN I BECAME PREGNANT with my son, I thought it was marvellous. Swollen feet, an appetite of six large men, heartburn, flatulence and a figure the same shape and consistency as a boiled dumpling ... but all worth it, as I had a new life growing in my tummy.

I was incredibly protective, stopped smoking (well, at least for the nine months he was resident in my stomach), stopped drinking wine (only the occasional sip for medicinal purposes) and took to hitting people with my umbrella and screaming 'Are you trying to hurt my baby?!' if they came within two feet of my belly. I was absolutely delighted when the small boy was born, since I felt I could now return to smoking 20 a day, having my wine on tap, or intravenously by drip, and thought that I would now have endless fun cooing at this small bundle, whilst people called by with wonderful presents.

Unfortunately, I hadn't really counted on the fact that he wouldn't want his eight hours sleep, same as me, that he might object to wine in his breast milk or that he might insist on my undivided attention all day, every day.

Despite this inauspicious start (when my son didn't really seem to grasp that mummy had her own needs) it's turned out rather well. When he was five, he said, 'Mummy, you know everything'. When he was twelve, he said 'Mummy, you don't know a lot do you?' Now he's fifteen, he views me rather as one would an old maiden aunt ... with deep affection, mild disdain and pity as I seem to have lost the plot rather in my advancing years. Despite his view that I probably know nothing and never did, he does condescend to humour me, tells me all his secrets and is rather affectionate. Most importantly, he understands that mummy's word is law and to think otherwise would place him in mortal danger from 'She who must be obeyed'. His Godmother thinks he's a 'cool dude' and I agree that he's pretty all right. He's also spectacularly handsome and I am quite prepared – actually, I feel it's my duty – to beat girls off him with a large stick. I have purchased one for just this purpose, so girls beware. I fully intend to be an absolute nightmare of a mother-in-law for any woman who gets past my vetting process (being able to stand after I've knocked her down a few times) and I'm quite looking forward to meddling in her life and being an absolute nuisance. Well, no girl's ever going to be quite good enough are they???

I also now have a marvellous daughter and, since I knew from previous experience that she was going to take away my liberty, I behaved much as one would when faced with their own mortality and sunk into depression before the event. Eventually, I rallied and viewed my increasing girth with glee, began brandishing my umbrella again at unsuspecting commuters who crossed my path, gave up smoking for the requisite nine months, ate until I could no longer distinguish between my chin and my neck and embraced heartburn as a long-lost friend.

Incredibly, despite my bad attitude and, frankly, bad behaviour during the pregnancy, she's turned out rather well. She is a mini version of me. Whilst this pleases me, it can put dread into the heart of any casual visitors, since she is hyper critical and has a tendency to start sentences with 'Now, I'm not being rude, but....' before telling me that her cousin ate the last biscuit without asking or put the plates back in the wrong cupboard. She is also the most affectionate child I have ever met. When she was little, I had to stop her flinging herself into the arms of the postman and going home with him, just because he looked a little bit sad and she thought she could cheer him up. The postman was a little bemused, but game – after all, she is very cute. My daughter has already learnt to flirt and considers, at ten years old, that it is important to get the bottom wiggle just right. She is slightly obsessed with breasts and keeps asking me when hers are 'going to get big like yours mummy', but I have explained that developing a magnificent bust like my own takes time and energy. Thankfully, she doesn't really think boys are quite the thing. She did have a boyfriend, but told him he was dumped during assembly as he was less than honest.... She is still very content with her dolly at the moment, and so her father is safe from having a heart attack at the thought of 'boys' just yet....

When my son was little, he would burst into tears if I told him that I was 'disappointed' in him, because he is keen to be amenable. My daughter views my disappointment as being somewhat self-indulgent on my part and will regard me for a moment or two, suggest a punishment and then ask if she can finish watching her TV programme, 'now please mummy'.

My son is regarded as 'cool like that' and my daughter is 'Miss Drama'. People ask me if I will ever have any more children and I say 'No, I am beyond child-bearing years'. That's not strictly true, but I'm not going to try and replicate perfection......

MIDDLE AGED, OR SOMETHING LIKE IT

———— ⟨∾⟩ ————

I WENT TO BOOK CLUB a few weeks ago and discovered that I appear to be approaching middle age, and I appear to be enjoying it!! This is something of a shock to my system, since I had thought that I was still very much a spring chicken – slightly worn about the edges, but definitely with a spring in my step.

Generally, book club is a time when we get to enjoy ourselves and pontificate long and hard on the merits of the book of the month. We enjoy arguing with each other about the author's meaning, the character, plot, sub plot, language and all manner of lovely lofty ideas, before we get stuck into the wine and begin shouting 'God you're so thick, of course the author didn't mean that you rank idiot', or hurling missiles at each other because we were interrupted when we were just getting into our stride.

On this occasion, it seems that I instigated a discussion with my fellow book club members on domesticity and we engaged in lively debate on the merits of washing powder, how frequently we clean our homes, the merits of the butcher as opposed to Tesco's meat. We also uttered obscene phrases like 'value for money' and 'you can't beat Tesco's chicken for flavour'.

I have been very busy depressing the hell out of myself by thinking about going to the gym in the hopes of getting what I thought was the inner me (young, feisty, flamboyantly sexy) to look like the outer me, (round, jowly, dull looking). Well, I may be too late, as I now appear to have descended into the depths of thinking a discussion on the merits of Tesco versus Iceland is riveting, and I am clearly approaching my dotage with impressive speed.

Unfortunately, it seems that I am missing Bert. I think I equate smoking with being rebellious and rebelliousness with being young, so that now I no longer smoke I think that I can't be as rebellious as I used to be.

I started smoking as a teenager, armed with all the tools to be outrageously oppositional. I revelled in it, enjoyed people's perception of me as being lawless. When Bert and I met, we weren't sure we liked each other. I thought he was a bad lad and he thought I was a bit of a wimp. He got around a bit and my friends had all had a go, but they made him sound so exciting that I thought I would try him out...

One by one, my friends drifted away from him and Bert and I were left alone to begin our love affair. I realised in the end that Bert was very controlling and, being rebellious, I rebelled. But the pull of him was so strong, he soon had me back in his grip. In the end, I couldn't do without him. My health suffered a bit, my children complained, my sister Maya refused to visit, claiming that he was a bad influence. But my love endured and we carried on for over twenty six years. Now, I've kicked him out, and I still miss him.

I don't think I'm ready for middle age cos I still have the urge to thwart authority, make outrageous and inappropriate comments, laugh loudly in church during a solum sermon, flirt with wild abandon whenever the mood takes me, drink rum and wine for the joy of getting drunk, wear skirts up around my thighs and display my chest with the least provocation... So, I've decided not to become middle aged just yet as I still have an awful lot of bad behaviour left in me.

A friend told me that 60 is the new 50, 50 is the new 40 and 40 is the new 30. Well, if that's the case, and everyone else is regressing at such an alarming rate, I think I'll join them.

PHARMACIST

TODAY, I WENT INTO work and left my patch at home! I spent the next two hours trying to find a chemist, a drug pusher, small child with a habit, anyone who could give me a patch quickly, with no questions asked. I advised my manager that I needed to leave the building to go and find a 'patch or a cigarette, NOW' and that if I were thwarted in my attempts, lives would indeed be at stake. He urged me to leave the building quickly. 'Run, don't walk – yes come back whenever you feel ready – really there's no rush' he said.

The pharmacist was an obliging bloke, but became alarmed when I told him to 'Open the box, give me a patch now and fill in the form in your own time, all right mate?' He quickly realised that I wouldn't be trifled with, but looked slightly apprehensive when I simultaneously slapped on the patch, chewed four pieces of nicotine gum and took a drag from the inhalator. Thankfully, the rush was immediate and I was able to apologise to the woman I had elbowed on the way into the shop, apologise for slapping the small boy who had previously hindered my path to the pharmacist, and proceeded to pick up and re-arrange the mountain of toiletries I had flung to the floor in my haste.

CHAPTER 5: WHO WAS I HURTING?

SOMETIMES, I FORGET why I decided not to smoke . I mean I know that I will prolong my life, blah, blah, blah ... that I can buy more shoes, lipsticks, blah, blah, blah ... but who was I hurting? Well ... me obviously, but I don't mind. I mean, so what if Bert cuts five years off my life, gives me horrible breath and a house that smells like an ashtray, no money, no shoes and constantly shunned by society for my unsociable *habit*. When I think about it, surely, I could have taken less drastic action..... cut down on non-essentials like food or clothing for instance. Yes, ok this may seem ridiculous .....but in the wee small hours when I'm yearning for Bert, this all makes marvellous sense......

THE JOY OF SHOES

SINCE MY PRIMARY MOTIVATION for giving up smoking was to buy more shoes, etc, I decided to talk it over with my favourite blue stiletto heeled shoes yesterday, but she was less than useless and kept wanting to talk about where we were going and the cupboard being dusty, which brought on her asthma. Shoes really are very stupid creatures and have nothing really to say for themselves. Sure, they look pretty, but you really can't get a good dialogue going and they are absolutely rubbish at giving advice, as they're really very insular and will only talk at boring length about themselves and how shiny they are. My boots are equally useless and are generally very macho individuals, given to long pauses and pontificating on the merits of long bracing walks, only getting really excited about the notion of a good hike. Unfortunately, neither my shoes nor my boots cared a hoot for my predicament and eyed me with disdain when I began to bemoan the loss of Bert.

I have tried talking to people about my loss, but they just smile at me and say, 'Aren't you good!' 'Don't worry the craving will pass'. Well-meaning, I know, but not much use when I'm eying them up and imagining they are an extra tall, extra broad cigarette......

I QUITE LIKE MYSELF

SINCE I WAS NO LONGER enjoying my daily cigarette, I wondered if I might have the puff for the gym and grimly decided to give it a go.

I am frankly surprised that I am even considering doing this...Running on the spot and getting sweaty (not in the good way).

When I separated from my second husband two years ago, I inadvertently appear to have given him the best years of my thighs, my stomach and my chin, whilst I was busy keeping house and minding the children. Dear Diary, if my eyes begin to glaze over you will understand that my thoughts went to that bad place of their own accord and I am trying to drag them back before they commit a heinous crime.

I remember, when I became newly single I was filled with joy, because everything smelt fresher, I wanted to lick the sky, roll about in the grass and jump for the sheer pleasure of it. I smiled all the time and thought that life was the most marvellous adventure. I went out with friends and treated each new experience like a wonderful gift, just for me. When I went out, I rocked with raucous laughter, because I was single and it was perfect. I wasn't interested in men and so they were interested in me. I clocked up an amazing amount of dates, discovered lust and acted in a reckless and abandoned fashion

In any event, suffice to say, I have several reasons for wanting to create a new and improved version of me. I have vague memories of someone who looked quite like me having arms and legs, which didn't wobble when she walked, a belly that I couldn't shake like a bowl full of jelly, or a face that didn't look as if I was secreting two small mice in each cheek. I quite like myself, and on good days, I thoroughly enjoy myself. But ... on those bad, bad days, I can – and do – make myself feel sick. Especially, if I come across myself suddenly in the mirror, recoil in horror and can't tear my eyes away from the carnage that is my stomach and thighs.

GYM FEVER ... OR NOT

SO I JOINED THE GYM – I cast aside all shame, donned the big knickers and stuffed the fat into their forgiving Lycra, squeezed into a pair of ailing jogging bottoms, brushed the lint and cobwebs from my trainers and sailed forth to do battle with the bulge.

My greeter gushed and flattered and lied and promised that for the miserly sum of a time share in Spain, I, too, could have thighs as small as a child's, no bottom to speak of, perched precariously above these thighs, and a stomach that I could bounce pennies off. I knew she was lying ... she knew that I knew that she was lying, but we agreed that, for my sanity's sake (and her commission), we would just continue to grin manically at each other and pretend.

I had a notion that you can wake up one morning and just pop down to the gym, but I was wrong, as you have to be prepared in mind as well as body. The people at the gym don't play and you need to make sure that you're ready to face the stares, the disdain and know the rules. Rules, yep there are rules... I had thought that you just get on the damn bike thing and pedal or walk about on that silly standing still machine that takes you nowhere, but nope I was wrong, wrong, wrong........

First you need the correct gear, so that you don't die of shame when all the other 'proper' gym going folk come in with their proper stuff. Checklist - Do you have your water bottle? This is not for quenching thirst, this is for holding in your hand and showing that you know that water is an important part of the 'look'. Do you have your towel? This is not to wipe sweat, sweat is not to be wiped, the more sweat you have the better. It shows that you worked very hard and are (almost) equal to the regular gym-going folk. You can wear manky sweats, but only if you really plan to sweat because then they will overlook your outfit as they can tell you're serious. If you only intend to perspire, you need Lycra leggings, a matching t-shirt and good trainers, preferably a hair band to hold the sweat out of your eyes and a stop-watch thingy that shows you're still breathing. Well, I think that's what it's for. I am not proper gym-going folk, so I don't really know.

Second, you need to perfect your nonchalant walk and look as if you know what each piece of machinery is for. If you look lost or confused, people will not help you. They will regard you as a hick from the sticks and look at you with all the disdain that you rightfully deserve. They will not generally laugh at you, but may look as if they are about to.

Then you need to remember not to ogle, huff, blow steam out of your ears or roar, 'Will you put some flipping clothes on' when the naked ladies wander around in the buff in the changing rooms, for all the world as if they were at home in their own bedrooms. I must confess, that I have found this step somewhat difficult, but have made huge efforts not to glare at people (anymore), purse my lips, swear loudly or turn away with great sighs of disgust. This is not easy, and I am unsure how much longer I can reign in my natural urges and not shout out 'cover yourself woman – I don't want to see your bits ... I have my own!!'

GYM VETERAN

I AM NOW A VETERAN of three days and am now able to meet other gym goers eyes. I am equipped with my water bottle (Sprite bottle with the label torn off), my gym clothes – well my son's. I now know what each piece of equipment is for, and can take off my top (leaving my bra on – nakedness does not have to be shared with strangers!!) without closing the cubicle curtains.

I walk on the spot, ride my bike to nowhere, pump weights for my thighs – and is all this making any difference? Well, I can't see any real changes but I feel stronger and I've now got a bit of a hobby, albeit one that makes me so bored I could eat my own arm for the entertainment value. But I've promised myself someone else's body for summer, so I'm gonna keep at it....

MAN ABOUT THE PLACE

SMOKING TAKES UP AN inordinate amount of time, and since I am in the throes of giving up, I am once again contemplating acquiring a man about the place, hence my recent foray back into online dating. I have been so busy trying not to smoke that talking nicely to strange men online was beyond me and I did find I was snarling rather than smiling.....sooooo not a good look....Anyhoo, now might be the time....

When I was sixteen, I had my first boyfriend. He was a delightful lad, full of youthful optimism and just this side of drop dead gorgeous. I had the usual teenage angst about whether he truly, truly loved and adored me and spent endless hours thinking about when he last kissed me, hugged me, bought me sweets. All marvellous harmless fun. Of course, we didn't go on to have children and he can remain forever in my mind as a wonderful boyfriend and I need not cast aspersions on his character. I would quite like one of those men, if at all possible, preferably with a side of fries and a rum cocktail...

BABY FEVER

I STARTED SEE A VERY nice man last week, own teeth, nice hair, GSOH, sexy bad, etc, etc, but unfortunately, it's not going to last, since he has no children and the mere thought of becoming a mummy to a small baby, who might require my undivided attention, fills me with unadulterated terror. No amount of begging and pleading on his part (he hasn't started begging yet, but no doubt this will come – I am, after all, a marvellous mummy!!), will do any good. I must stand firm, no indecision, assert my rights as a woman to reclaim my body for my own enjoyment, my evenings for my own entertainment and my fridge for wine (and the odd meal for my children). Wine needs room to breathe and cannot be contaminated by baby bottles. Baby bottles filled with formula talk to you when you open the fridge. They grin at you stupidly, eyeing your less-than-svelte figure with ill-concealed glee. They say, 'Oh don't you want one of us now? No? Baby not hungry? Ah well, she will be in a minute. No, no need to close the door, you'll only have to open it again in a sec, since she's bound to want her feed ... any second now.'

Now, don't mistake me, I quite like my children and – in small doses – they're really rather enjoyable, but I insist on spending 'quality' time with them and I am quite happy to growl, in Greta Garbo fashion, 'I want to be alone' when they are no longer amusing me. I do recall that, when they were small, they did not grasp the notion of mummy 'wanting to be alone' and whilst I was happy to accept that their understanding may have been limited (due to their years), I was not always best pleased to have my sleep interrupted, baby sick adorning all my clothes, a stomach and nether regions stretched to all hell, and a full frontal lobotomy, which impeded my thought processes and made me incapable of holding onto the thread of any conversation that did not include the words, 'baby sick, sleepless nights, colic, dummies, breast or bottle!!'

Just to underline my terror, I woke up the other night after having a dream that I was – once again – 'with child'. I staggered from the bedroom, wild about the eyes, threw back a glass of rum, lifted my nightdress to confirm that there wasn't a child lurking about my nether regions and about to burst forth from my 'private place' and made frantic calls to my friend Lorena, asking her to confirm that I wasn't 'with child'. Thankfully, she was very helpful, swore at me soundly and at great length for waking her, told me to 'get a grip', explained that no one with any brain cells at all would wish to impregnate and asked me not to call her again until I had at least recovered some of my senses.

So, on balance, I think that my family may be complete ... and if I ever say any different I have instructed my brother, Emmanuel, that he has leave to deposit me at the nearest mental institution, since I will, almost certainly, have lost my mind.

FROGS IN KINGS' CLOTHING

I AM ALREADY FED UP with dating, as its sooooo hard, but I'm not done yet, so persevere I will. I've had remarkable bad luck with the last few dates and really some of them need to stop wasting good air by continuing to breathe. I mean – seriously – I have, on occasion, barely escaped with my life as there are some nut, nut nutty folk out there.

Anyway, the reason for my slight case of misery gutsitis, is because of a man. Well, it wouldn't be anything else would it? Nothing useful like concern about famine, world hunger, pestilence or poverty ... no, just a crappy man.

What was so annoying about this Adonis – and, trust me, he was an Adonis – was that he masqueraded as a really great guy, with kingly attributes and tricked me into thinking 'Wahay! Your lucks in there girl!!'

He was older (well 47), which I thought meant mature. He was pretty in a square-jawed masculine kinda way ... with a deep voice, big chest, and wonderful rock-hard thighs ... ooh, just wonderful. He had a good job, was nice to children and animals, had his own home....tick box, tick box, tick box.

Anyway, after lulling me into a false sense of security – refusing to allow me to carry bags, use public transport, go out without him, cross the road without his support – he suddenly became an irritating moody bollocks. It was most disconcerting and I tried ... I *really* tried to cheer him up, did cartwheels, got up to cook in the middle of the night, told knock-knock jokes, all to no avail. And when I got really fed up and criticised the big old misery guts, he got all upset and did a Houdini on me.

And the moral of my story? Well, there ain't one!! Ha! People can make up their own bloody moral ...

.... Well, all right then, the moral is ... frogs can – and do – like to play dress up. And their favourite game is 'pretend to be a King', so we have to be careful that the 'King' is a King and we don't end up dating pond life.

NO REAL WHOOSH!

AFTER MR 47, I MET and dated a really, really nice guy. I am really racking up the dates, but I have no time to waste ... I and 43 and a bit now!

He wasn't the prettiest baby, but he didn't have a face that would scare you. And, anyway, I had decided to stop being so shallow after my encounter with Mr 47...

Anyway, we got on really well. He was great to be around ... good conversation, good company, friendly, funny and a really – very special – kisser. I could have kissed him for hours. I felt like I was meandering in a corn field, but sadly, there was no real whoosh, and he had to go.

DATING OR SOMETHING LIKE IT

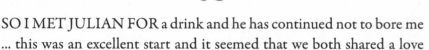

SO I MET JULIAN FOR a drink and he has continued not to bore me
... this was an excellent start and it seemed that we both shared a love
of drink. His tipple was brandy and mine is rum, so we bonded over
describing the taste and texture of our favourites.

He was remarkably easy on the eye, laughed at my jokes, paid
for my meals and drove me home like a gentleman. There was a very
naughty glint in his eye and, therefore, gentlemanly behaviour may not
have always been on the cards, but I appreciated the effort.

SIX MONTHS AND COUNTING

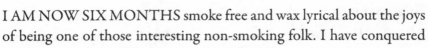

I AM NOW SIX MONTHS smoke free and wax lyrical about the joys of being one of those interesting non-smoking folk. I have conquered my addiction to cigarettes and feel invincible.

Bert no longer talks to me and, when I go into the newsagents, he turns away and pretends to be perusing the car magazines. I know he can't drive, so he's fooling no one. I feel a tinge of sadness, but he was a really bad friend and I'm so glad I realised that before he succeeded in killing me.

I am quite boring on the subject of my marvellousness and lie beautifully whenever I am asked if it was hard to give up smoking. 'No ... no, not at all!' I announce gaily, but never in the presence of my sisters, the dry cleaners, Rosalyn, the chemist or my children, as they know that, errrrm, I was a tad overwrought on occasion.

I have sunken quite happily into the arms of rum, wine and cream buns and I know that, one day, these friends will have to leave me too, but not yet!

CHAPTER 6: TWELVE WEEKS TO SKINNY

DEAR DIARY,

It has been the best few years of my life! I've stopped smoking, stopped drinking, bought more shoes and met the love of my life!

I decided to write a whole other diary for the stop drinking journey, as you dear diary are far too delicate for all of that!

I'm not sure that I'm actually divorced from my first husband yet, but this is a minor inconvenience and, since I do not plan to commit bigamy, I will definitely contact the court and just check that the decree absolute was granted, as prison grey will not suit my colouring.

I feel remarkably full of vigour at 49, but I am still a bit rounder than I had hoped and, since we're

getting married very soon, I have twelve weeks to get from curvy to skinny!

Himself says that he is delighted with me as I am, and is keen for me to continue cooking my gastronomic delights. But I've assured him that I will continue making him salmon wellington, and the only stomach that will suffer is mine.

FAT AS A FOOL

IN MY EARLY 40S, I decided that I was as fat as a fool and twice as funny looking. It came to me in a flash, that I had allowed my belly to overtake my thighs ... (again), my cheeks resembled mountains of gobstoppers, and I was reasonably sure that the folds of my chin might soon obscure my neck if I was not careful.

This descent into fatdom has been slow, but I did put my back into it. I've ensured that I've consumed crisps in vast quantities and washed them down with vats of red wine and rum. I've eaten late, stuffed down ice cream and sandwiches, revelled in potatoes and guzzled on cheese sandwiches. I haven't neglected a single part of my anatomy and I have been scrupulously fair about distributing the fat equally liberally over my face, my bottom, my breasts and my thighs. So I wibbled and wobbled delightfully when I walked, much like an erupting bowl of trifle.

My epiphany came on a trip to Ireland. I was overexcited since I love the accents and was keen on meeting up with more Irish folk who might allow me to partake in the craic. I entered a store, and discovered that the only thing I could purchase in the clothing store was a hat or a woolly scarf. This distressed me, and, whilst I wanted to slap the assistant silly and demand to know why they didn't cater for the more rotund patron, I duly accepted that this was a designer store, which meant that they make clothes for skinny people. Those folk who shiver in the summer because their bones are barely covered in flesh, whose skin is pulled tight against the sinew and muscle with no cushion of fat in between, no soft folds... those people I want to emulate. So I looked longingly at the wonderful dresses, fingered the sumptuous fabric of the coats, sighed deeply and left.

I promised myself – there and then – that I would be thin and return triumphantly to that shop and buy, oooh at least six dresses. Of course, I may need to do a quick bank job in between just to get the cash, cos those prices were eye wateringly high.

Anyhoo, I came home and embraced the no food diet. Seriously, this diet says, 'Hey fool, you know you're fat right? Well now we're gonna starve you, ya great lump. You wanna make something of it??? Well do ya? No, I thought not, you great lump of lardy arse.' This diet is extremely rude, but I don't dare answer back cos I need to lose weight ... and I'm a wimp. My resolve did waiver when everyone kept telling me that this diet was gonna kill me, leave me bald, trembling, shaking, with bad breath too. But I am very used to ignoring bad news, so I ignored 'em. All I knew was that this diet promised to make me a shadow of my former self within three months, so I embarked on it with high hopes, so what's a little hair loss, high blood pressure, and bad breath compared to being skinny?

So you basically get powdered packets that you add water to. When I mixed my first packet and ate it, I promptly threw up, so I thought ... oh right, so this is the vomiting diet. But no, my consultant assured me that this wasn't the desired outcome, so I was limited to shakes and bars, since I couldn't eat the other stuff. I was almost always constantly hungry and had vivid dreams about cheese sandwiches, who jeered at me when I refused to eat them. But I began to see my cheekbones, my shoulder bones and my neck, so I kept doing it. I even gave up the drink, for a time....

I had a pictures of a slimmer, younger me taped to my fridge and fully intended to reclaim the bone structure and skin tone of that woman. My breasts would never be that pert again ... damn they were great. I could almost take someone's eye out. But getting those thighs back was a definite possibility – and I did it, three times! I lost three stone three times! But, as soon as I started eating normally again I was, once again, as fat as a fool.

FAMILY SAY THE NICEST THINGS

---※◎※---

I VIVIDLY REMEMBER my first holiday to Jamaica a few years ago. I was greeted at the airport by my cousin, who hadn't seen me for some years. 'Oh my, oh my ...' he exclaimed, 'but lawd, you fat, you fat you fat!!' Laughing hysterically in between pronouncements of fatness and seemingly delighted with my enlarged proportions, he proceeded to proudly tell my relations, gathered at the airport to greet me, that I had put on weight and was now fat! It felt churlish to be upset by his comments since he was clearly ecstatic!

I was perhaps less than delighted, as I was on round four or was it round sixteen of my diet journey. I'd tried the very low calorie diet (VLCD). I'd tried the 'eat away your Syns diet'. I'd tried food combinations and juice fasts with varying degrees of success.

I'd also tried the – stay as you are, you gorgeously voluptuous goddess diet – but, unfortunately, I never really got that one, so the search for slimming potions and quick fixes continued.

Over the years, I've had some success and was suffused with elation when people looked at me sideways and wondered, with brows furrowed, whether I was too thin. When matronly aunts squeezed my cheeks and suggested that I eat a dumpling or two, in order to put some weight on those bones, I could have melted into a puddle of joy! But skinny me never lasted, because as soon as I reached the dizzying heights of being skinny, I would commence operation stuff my face! Simply because I am like a marauding ninja eating machine! Nothing is safe ... my children's left-overs, mine. My sister's dinner, mine! And woe betide anyone getting in the way of my eating.

For every diet I embarked on, I never actually bothered to listen to talk about portion control or eating in moderation, as I was too busy trying to stop myself starving and feeling deprived of everything I held dear!

HEY GIRL

I WENT TO A FUNCTION last week and everyone kept saying, 'Hey, Girl, looking good!!' I saw the pictures and all I could think was 'Hey Girl, looking fat!!'

I was making jokes about my double chins, asking to be photographed in soft focus, or for my chins to be airbrushed out, but it ain't funny. It's a crying shame that I would allow my face, my body, my legs – which used to stop traffic, well they did, – to go to hell in a hand basket like this.

BIRTHDAY JOY

HAPPY BIRTHDAY TO ME! How the hell did I turn 50 years old! Gosh age is so sneaky. There I was minding my own business, feeling 28 and marvellous, when bam! Suddenly I was flipping middle aged.

Whilst my hair is more salt than pepper, I am loving my bottom skimming plaits and big sis says I look rock-chick(ish), so I love that.

I know that I was rather determined to grow old disgracefully, and had fully intended rocking up in heaven all used up, worn out and with a huge beatific grin of self-satisfaction on my face – content that I had lived my life at breakneck pace!

I am reliably informed that I don't look my age and that the years of smoking, drinking and eating indulgently have barely left their mark. This is sooooo not true, but I am happy to pretend and have become adept at slapping on make-up and hiding fat – now you see it, now you don't.

Yesterday, Himself described me as petite and said that he could easily pick me up and pop me in his pocket. I told him I had no objections to this and would nestle there quite happily if he fed me biscuits and cake.

When I woke up this morning, I looked in the mirror and noticed that my skin remains unlined! Thank you very much. And whilst I am slightly curvy, well, all right, leaning towards Fatty McFattyville, this is not my fault, as sweets, cakes and biscuits are delicious and they keep appearing in my cupboards as if by divine hand. Well, I know I bought them, but what can I do? They insisted. They called me from the shelves and threw themselves in kamikaze fashion into my basket ... so I was powerless to resist ... I am only flesh and blood dammit.

Mummy's angel baby, first fruit of my loins, called me this morning and wished me a happy birthday. 'Mummy, one of things I love about you is that you continue to change and grow as you get older.' He said. That's so lovely, and I am so pleased I had him ... months of gut-wrenching heartburn, unfeminine flatulence, and 11 hours of excruciating labour were all worth it for this moment. I was delighted that now he had reached the grand old age of 22, I appeared to have redeemed myself.

Mummy's second baby, second fruit of my loins, loves birthdays. When I moan about wearing yet another gargantuan badge proclaiming my age to the world, she says 'Hello! Who had a party every single year for me and Callum's birthday? Every ... single ... year! And you insisted on inviting everyone we know?' I caved, since I really do love a birthday, but just cannot cope with the badges. Since I am the author of her all-consuming interest in birthdays, I try to give in with good grace. She insisted I wear the huge badge she presented me with. I promised to wear it, but I don't want to and may sulk. I'm going to try a sneaky way to avoid wearing it. I am likely to be unsuccessful, as I know she will be watching me with hawk-like attention.

Today, I marvelled at just how marvellous I am because I made these fabulous children. I know their fathers had a hand in it somewhere, but really it was all me! Me! Me! I really enjoy them, well most of the time ... and since they left their sticky stage behind, I am really rather delighted with them! Particularly when they come to visit me. They say they missed me and need mummy hugs, but then they make a beeline for the fridge and the tumble dryer, so they're fooling no one.

Callum is so wonderfully nerdy, and has everlasting patience with his increasingly eccentric mummy. He is the most loving young man I know and he is my favourite son! I only have one, so it is rather convenient that he is my favourite since I don't have a spare son.

Iris is mummy's baby, 'my wash belly' as granny would say. She is such a treat, kind to strangers, given to cuddling, has a heart that overflows for everyone, given to foisting birthday badges on all and sundry and has the moral compass of a nun! As a child, I remember that she was forever doing up my buttons, whilst crying 'Cover yourself mummy!' when I dared to bare cleavage! In fairness, I was almost naked in my 20s and 30s and my favourite outfit was a pair of Daisy Duke shorts and knee-high stiletto boots.

I may have missed my calling as a madame ...

Daddy called me, bright and early, and asked, 'Were you sleeping?' but this would hardly matter to daddy, since he is of the view that sleep is overrated and that his telephone calls should always be answered immediately, since he is 86 years old, and ... well ... just because. He sang me happy birthday. Awwww, I was so touched that he a) remembered, since he has nine children, eighteen grandchildren and six great grandchildren, so he is forgiven, and b) that he sang! The patriarch of the family, the convivial host, the stern voice of reason and the naughtiest one of us all. I do adore him and have tried very hard to emulate his parenting style, with varying degrees of success. I tried telling my children off in his imitable style when they were little, but they just rolled around on the floor laughing and it just didn't work the same as when daddy used to do it. I don't think I had enough eye action, because the hard stare, like Paddington bear, was missing.

Himself presented me with birthday flowers in bed. Awwww, he is so lovely. Well, he is when he isn't screaming at the telly when Arsenal is playing or devastating our kitchen! Is there anything worse than a chef who likes to cook at home, but forgets that he doesn't have a sous chef conveniently tucked away in the cupboard! That aside, he is absolutely gorgeous ... I love his twinkly eyes (they look so naughty). I love his legs, and I remember when we first started dating, he would run up to me and I would just stand and watch whilst this gorgeous ebony man – with grace and flow – ran to meet me. I love his head so much. Stroking his bald head is lovely, as it's so delightfully round and squidgy ...

I love lying in and not going to work. Not listening to silly people say stupid things on my birthday is my gift to myself. I nestled down under my covers and opened the family WhatsApp page, where my entire gaggle of sisters and brothers, nieces, nephews and cousins had wished me happy birthday. It's so marvellous to wake up to this much love and attention. I'm feeling truly blessed with my family, whom I love dearly. I'm delighted that, when we left our childhood behind, we stopped thumping each other and we're actually really rather respectable now – and quite nice to each other! I am, frankly, astonished that we all have respectable jobs because we were exceptionally naughty children.

VOMIT TIME

I REMEMBER WHEN I WAS 10 years old, I realised that if I ate Mars Bars, KP crisps and Belgian buns and then threw up, I would never put any weight on. I have absolutely no idea why weight was even an issue for me since I was devoid of puppy fat from early on. I can only assume that it was a by-product of my delightful precociousness, since I did rather revel in being rebellious and rather oppositional. Good times, good stuff. In later life, experts – and there have been many who have poked and prodded at my marvellous brain – have said I was trying to control something, which does rather make sense as I was constantly trying to extricate my wonderful mummy from the clutching tentacles of my – oh so annoying – siblings and I did spend my days day dreaming about being an only child.

Where was I? Oh yes, me and an iced Belgian bun hanging over the loo vomiting.

Little sis, Kiki heard me one day and told daddy. She was such a snitch and, if daddy hadn't been staring at me, I would have given her such a thump. But daddy had on his 'I will not be thwarted' face, so I gave him my attention. Yes, daddy I did vomit, I responded to his enquiry, but it was an accident. 'Ok', said daddy, with a hard stare. 'Are you planning to do it again?'

'No daddy', says I, and he says, 'Ok then ... make sure', accompanied by a very hard stare.

And that was the end of my bulimic journey. Truth be told, I'd been doing this for months, and if Kiki hadn't told, and my compulsion had been stronger than my dad's wrath, I may have been bingeing and purging to this day.

I think that's when my complex relationship with food began ... I'm not sure. Although, it may have had something to do with Johnny, the boy next door. I remember Johnny was a horrible boy, but I was fascinated with him, as he was white, pimply and had shocking ginger hair. I was used to boys who looked like my brothers and cousins, with brown eyes like mine, curly black hair and varying shades of chocolatey brown skin, so Johnny was fascinating with his translucent marshmallow white and pink skin, freckles and abundance of pimples.

I remember he showed me his willy one day. I recoiled in horror, particularly, as he proceeded to wave it about. I was fearful that this funny pink thing was going to get me. Once he had it safely tucked away, he then asked me to show him mine, but since I didn't have a willy, I patiently explained that I would be unable to comply with his request. It soon became apparent that he wanted me to show him my 'area', which mummy had been clear was not to be shown to anyone and had painstakingly explained that it was only to be uncovered for wee wees, poo poos and vigorous washing. I told Johnny that he was a 'horrible boy', thumped him and told on him to my mummy. I remember watching mummy stand up straight with this serious look on her face, before telling me to 'come on', as she was going to see his mummy. Oooooh, I remember thinking. He's gonna get it now. He had made mummy mad. Mummy knocked on his mummy's front door and she was magnificent. 'Mrs W', she said 'Johnny has been very naughty!' Ooooh, she was using her posh Jamaican accent. 'He tried to h'inveigle mi daughter to show him her underneat and he showed her him tings, now I don't know, which part him learn such disgustingness from, but I beg yuh mek sure him never h'ask her nothin again, as mi and yuh will fall out'. Mrs W tried to defend Johnny and said she was sorry, but when she shut the door I heart her slap him and heard him squeal. I was delighted. Mummy patted me, gave me a cuddle, said I was a good girl and gave me cake. Since it wasn't my birthday, it wasn't the weekend and no one was celebrating I realised that cake was my reward for being a good girl and it was such a lovely comforting feeling.

I think I have constantly tried to replicate that feeling, but cake has never felt that good again.

SCHOOL DAZE

MY DAUGHTER IS GOING to secondary school soon, and we recently went to visit her new school, which is my old school. I remembered the school motto and chanted it with her, demonstrating some pride, which is odd since I definitely recall not giving a damn about the school motto when I was actually going to school.

She asked me whether I was happy at school and I said, 'Yes, darling. It was marvellous ... best years of my life!' This was not strictly true, but when faced with her eyes staring up at me apprehensively, and almost begging, I found I couldn't really say anything else!

I mean, I did enjoy school, you understand ... I just couldn't stand most of the other pupils and would have cheerfully put out a contract on most of the teachers!

I did have some incredible friends whilst at school, Audrea and Brooke are still my favourite lunch companions, but I had an unfortunate habit of referring to some of the girls as 'man beasts', since they wore their navy-blue box pleated skirts, wonderfully accessorised with their trainers! In fact I judge them for not wanting to beat me up more! In the end, I think they cultivated me, because I could show them how to wear high heels and stuff their bras and I cultivated them, because they were bigger than me and could fight on my behalf! You see, I had an unfortunate habit of running off at the mouth and not having anything to back it up with!!

The friendships you make at school are incredibly enduring and no friendship you make before or after is really quite the same. There is something about the relationships made in our formative years – when we're really coming to grips with who we are – that have this depth of intimacy and realism that may be missing in later friendships. I have been incredibly blessed to meet and form friendships with some wonderful women over the years and, despite the challenges we've faced and sometimes divergent paths, I still consider that the 'girls' from school were pretty damn fantastic!

I recently met up with an old school friend and we exchanged numbers and chatted for hours on the phone. We hadn't seen each other for years, but secrets were exchanged, views given on how the other was managing their love lives, mortgages, and children and we both felt an absolute right to behave and communicate this way.

CHAPTER 7: MUMMY MEMORIES

Thinking about mummy yesterday made me think about her again today.

I remember when she died, and people kept saying 'Oh my god ... she was too young ... only 36'. At the time, I kept thinking, 'My mum has died and that really cannot be possible because I need her, she is my best friend, makes the best cake and taught me how to blow bubbles with chewing gum, but she wasn't young, so what on earth do they mean?' At sixteen, I thought 36 was sooooo old. Now from the vantage point of 50, I realise just how ridiculously young she was. Oh to be 36 again. Actually, scrap that, 36 was a yuck time. My ex-husband was being a horse's ass, I was spotty, and once I had put the children to bed, most of my evenings were spent drinking rum and moaning about my life. So 50 is waaaaaaaay better. But mummy was young, ridiculously young, unfinished, so much else to do, young.

I often think about what she would think of me now. Through the years, I imagined her saying 'For god's sake, will you put some clothes on!?' 'Where is the rest of the material for that skirt? I can see your bottom!' And when I had my children, I imagined her laughing and saying, 'You brute', when she noticed just how similar in temperament my small girl is to me and laughing with delight that I was about to get the same treatment as she did. More recently, I thought about how proud she would have been that I stopped smoking and drinking.

Dear Diary,

I haven't written that down in this diary. This needed a whole other book, not least because stopping drinking took me to a place that was difficult to write about. I think mummy would have been disappointed that cigarettes and alcohol had begun to mean so much to me, and if she heard me describe them as friends, she may have felt compelled to slap the taste out of my mouth. Mummy was old school and there was no crutch. There was just 'Get on and do it', 'Sort it out, make it happen and hurry up!'

THE JOY OF COLLEGE

I AM MIRED IN MEMORY right now and the memories are coming so thick and fast I can hardly write them quickly enough on to paper. It feels like my head is buried in treacle and every memory is coated in a thick unguent goo. I never access these memories and they are buried so deeply.

I remember, at college, dancing on the common room table when I should have been in my shorthand typing class. My tutor peeped in and shouted, 'Brown, get down off that table and get to class'. I ignored her, as my public were baying for me to sing 'silly games' again and my backing singers, Loretta and Martine were waiting for me... since myself and the singer Janet Kay were the only ones who could reach that high note, I felt it was my duty to ignore my tutor. I really could not be bothered to do anything that anyone asked me to do....oppositional me was in full effect, because I was so determined to hide the fact that I was grieving mummy and doing whatever I damn well pleased was working for me...

If I was naughty enough, outrageous enough and laughed at everything, I could pretend she was still here.

Although it was a bit of a surprise when they kicked me out of college – and no amount of 'but my mum just died miss', would cut it, since that had already excused me making my shorthand teacher cry, breaking the common room table with my vigorous dancing and having being caught having a marvellous kissing session with Simon when I should have been in my typing class – sadly my time was up. My three months in college were marvellous and I remember them with fondness, despite the fact that this was probably the point when my full-on descent into self-destruction began.

ALCOHOL, MY LOVE

I REMEMBER LEAVING college and discovering an all-consuming love of alcohol. It was naughty. It was freeing. It was delicious. And it was a wonderful antidote to grief. Cigarettes and rum became firm friends.

TV CRUSHES

I HAVE DECIDED THAT I want to get married again. I am actually still married, and I am planning to marry Himself, but this is a minor point and one that is easily overcome by virtue of a quickie divorce ... or I could try bigamy, since I understand that it is becoming fashionable for very busy people.

Anyway, I have decided that as well as marrying Himself, I want to marry Nick Vera from Cold Case. He is a white, wonderfully rotund gentleman, who is a homicide detective and works alongside Lily Rush, solving old homicide cases. On first glance, Nick looks misogynistic. He's possibly bigoted and definitely rude and forthright in his manner. But underneath it all, he's a big ole pussycat!! In recent months, I've found myself curled in my armchair, glued to the TV, not eating crisps, and beaming at him whenever he speaks. I have considered whether the onset of dementia is approaching and whether I am, in fact, losing my faculties, but I am strangely drawn to him.

He has a huge head of curly hair, marvellous Santa cheeks, crinkly eyes, a lovely round tummy and is just a huge bear of a man! I find that I am having to restrain myself from kissing the TV and keep saying, 'Ahh, isn't he lovely?' whenever he says anything ... anything at all! Last week he said, 'Our boy's back', when referring to a serial rapist and I was delighted with him. Yesterday, he said something equally profound and I just couldn't get enough. He's the kind a guy that sneeringly says, 'Suffragettes? What's that?' ... and then goes out and reads a book on suffragettes. He's just lovely and if I can manage to get a ticket to the US, look out Nick, here I come!!

Unfortunately, this is not the first time that I have had a crush on a TV personality, and I do have to consider whether I have a very slender grip on reality. That said, some TV characters are wonderfully three dimensional ... I am desperately trying to get others to join me in my madness. One of my earliest crushes was on a lad in his twenties, who appeared in East Enders. Sadly, my love affair ended when they killed him off in a road accident and my grief was overwhelming for at least the next two episodes. I was quite rightly ashamed of my passion.

I am very fair and am just as happy developing crushes on TV characters or characters in books. Sometimes, the depth of feeling I develop for a character in a book is amazing, since the characters I create in my mind far exceed any inexact representation that media moguls can conceive, and I can imbue my characters with all sorts of imaginary qualities!!

I remember enjoying the Rupert Campbell Black character in the Jilly Cooper novels. I longed to be graced with a disdainful glance or be on the receiving end of one of his lip curls. Or to be flung over his shoulder and ... hmmm...

I grew up with Mills and Boon novels – the plot is always the same, which is quite satisfying as you know what you're getting. Wonderfully macho and charismatic male meets wilting violet (wimp) female.

Wonderfully attractive female snags him first, and wilting violet doesn't think that she has a chance, cos he's awful to her and treats her like a serf. But in the end, he's forceful and dynamic and admits that he loves wilting violet and was fighting his love, hence being so awful to her! He declares his love in a wonderfully dramatic fashion and drop kicks wonderfully attractive woman out of bed!! Well, sort of.

Anyway, I love TV and books as they're marvellous escapism and can transport you to a world of unreality, with people that you can love or hate without consequence, and there's the joy.

Sometimes – just occasionally – reality Sucks!! So I will continue to escape into my TV or curl up with a good book.

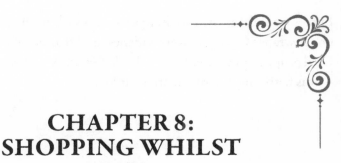

CHAPTER 8:
SHOPPING WHILST
FAT

I decided to go shopping today, despite the fact that shopping for clothes when you are rather rotund and a bit on the roly-poly side is a bit of a mission. Shoulders back, deep breaths and lots of 'You can do it' affirmations! Because it's soul destroying, always, all the time, forever.

I refuse to spend lots of money on clothes, because I am fairly sure that I will be the next size down by Sunday, so hardly seems worth it.

I loitered but eventually, basket in hand I wandered into the plus size section, whilst gazing mournfully at the skinny folk over in the skinny folk section, but dragged myself back to the task in hand, filling my basket with anything that says size 18 or 20. The colour, cut, design are irrelevant. The single criterion is 'Will it fit?!' I haven't been to Primani for some time and I know they have had a refit, but, when I went into the cubicle, I noticed one mirror in front of me and one mirror behind me! What new fresh hell is this?! Why do I want a mirror behind me? Who asked these shop fitter folk if I wanted to be confronted with a back view of my dimpled behind whilst trying on something new?! I angled my head to the side trying to avoid the eye of the mirror, who was sniggering quietly in the corner assuring me that she would see my bottom very soon.

After much exertion, I poked my head out in triumph and, whilst my plaits were sweaty and plastered across my forehead, I believed that

I was successful as the top fit. I gazed at myself in the mirror....back fat under wraps? Check. Covers wideness and flatness of bottom? Check. Covers upper and lower belly? Check. Great. Whether the top suits me – or is flattering – hardly matters. It fits.

PHOTOGRAPH HELL

'BUT WHY DO YOU WANT to take a photograph of me?' I asked my manager. 'I mean, I do realise that you want to let clients know who the staff team are, but why is this my business?!' She was really rather unreasonable and would not be persuaded that I was having a bad hair day, since my hair was looking pretty damn good, even if I say so myself.

I have spent so many years avoiding the camera because whilst I love to capture memories, I generally want to be the one behind the camera. This is because, when I see the photographs, an imposter will be wearing my clothes! Albeit with a wonderful sense of fashion and a startling resemblance to me, but there end all similarities. I'll be faced with an apparition purporting to be me, but sporting rather more chins than I thought I possessed, with the hip proportions of a sumo wrestler and the thighs of a champion disc thrower.

I stood in between two of my co-workers – a tip I learnt to disguise the width of my hips – and tried to make myself small.

THONG, THONG, THONG

I HAVE HEARD OF THONGS, I have sung the thong song, but I had never attempted to wear one. I normally pour my size 16/18 bottom into lovely comforting full briefs, that properly cover all my nether regions.

Today, I took a notion that I was missing out and so I gave in to peer pressure. Actually, why am I lying to myself? There was none. I just thought I was missing out. I went to an expensive lingerie store. I thought it's important to spend extra for a strong gusset, since there would be little material anywhere else.

I eyed these scraps of material and even the size 18s resembled a wisp of fabric, which did not look up the task of containing my generous proportions. This did nothing to assuage my concerns that thongs and their ilk were perhaps not for me. Undaunted, I surged ahead and I purchased a black scrap of fabric and returned home.

Well, I got my legs in, that part appears to work the same as my trusty comfy M&S knickers, but then horror of horrors the thong bit of this contraption disappeared up around my back bottom area and I had to pluck hard to retrieve it! What dastardly instrument of torture is this? Why is this contraption attempting to floss my nether regions? I tore off the offending garment, threw it to the ground and stamped on it for good measure. Ahhhhhh hellll no! I decreed – I would never assault my personage with this bottom flosser again!

CHAPTER 9:
NIRVANA

This morning, when I woke up, I fondled my stomach. 'Hello my lovely', I crooned. 'Aren't you round and squishy'. I do love the feel of my tummy. I just wish there was a little less of her.

Why is it Monday ... Again? Why do I have to go to work ... Again? Why am I not a lady of leisure? Why is Himself not rich? Life is sooooo unfair.

I tried to work, I really did. Well, all right I tried for an hour, then gave up and scanned Facebook.

I saw an advert for Slimpod. I eyed it with some suspicion, since it claimed that it wasn't a diet but it also claimed that one would lose weight effortlessly. Hmmmm, I wasn't sure it made sense, but the reviews were extraordinarily positive and I wasn't sure that this many folk could be lying. Well, actually, they could, but since there was a free trial, I signed up.

TREVOR, YOU SMOOTH TALKER YOU

FROM READING THE REVIEWS, I had heard about this Trevor fellow who, apparently, croons to you nightly from an audio recording. Himself was mildly put out that I was preparing to don ear phones and have sweet nothings whispered in my ear by someone who wasn't him, but I explained that Trevor was only talking to me about weight loss and did not have what Himself and I had. Appeased, Himself turned his attention back to the football and all was well ...

Anyway, I listened intently to Trevor who told me to imagine the me I wanted to see. I paraphrase, but I conjured up this powerful image of me in black skinny jeans, with a t-shirt tucked into the waist band and no cardigan to cover my lumps! Oooooh it was exciting...

ENERGISED AND READY

I JUMPED OUT OF BED, full of the joys of spring and painted my front garden wall. Himself was mightily impressed with my creativity, we had planned to knock it down, as it was pretty ugly.

My renewed energy levels are soaring, which is a welcome change, as lately I had taken to having a surfeit of cake and then lying prone on the sofa, refusing to move my feet and insisting that Himself's lap was the proper resting place for them, as they were so tired.

NO CAKE

LAST NIGHT IN BED, I suddenly sat bolt upright and shouted, '...but I didn't eat cake'. Himself was mildly annoyed at being rudely awoken and insisted I shut up and go back to sleep, but I insisted that he join me in marvelling at the fact that I hadn't had cake. Because he is quite, quite lovely, he told me that he was '...delighted with me', and that I was a 'veritable saint, full of restraint'. He then asked, 'Please can I go back to sleep now?' Since he had been so nice, I agreed, but lay awake thinking about the fact that I hadn't eaten cake for the first time in months! This was my daily ritual ... it was what I did ... get up, work, cook, eat dinner, eat cake ... crisps ... biscuits ... nuts....stuff....

I was in the presence of a miracle, as not only had I not eaten cake or any other deliciously sugary or fatty morsel, but I hadn't even noticed!

POLLYANNA, MY FRENEMY

WHEN I GAVE UP SMOKING, I named it. Smoking was called Bert. Bert was my ride or die friend, my there in my ups and my downs. Sure he tried to kill me a few times, but what's a little attempted murder between good friends?!

Therefore, in time-honoured tradition, I have named my addiction to snacks Pollyanna because she's perky, annoying, always upbeat, and always sees the bright side, even when she's in the midst of giving me sugar shock! It makes perfect sense to crave what I shouldn't have, because I have always done that, but now with the aid of my new friend Slimpod (SP), I can really kick the habit.

EXERCISE THE GATEWAY TO HELL

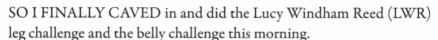

SO I FINALLY CAVED in and did the Lucy Windham Reed (LWR) leg challenge and the belly challenge this morning.

I Hate Exercise sooo much. Not normal run-of-the-mill dislike ... nope. It's all out hate! Exercise bores me so much that I would rather stick a fork in my eye for the entertainment value.

This Is A Big Deal!

In the spirit of fairness to myself, I'm counting the fact that I did this as a win, despite the fact that there is a distinct possibility that I may, in fact, be dead. Oh my lawd! I am seriously unfit!

I started with good intentions, clad only in my underwear, so I could see the body devastation up close and remember why I was attempting to kill myself with exercise.

I started off well, and then found I was puffing like a train, roaring like a saw and was becoming rather red in the face! I tried to breathe normally, as she suggested, but I flipping couldn't! Steam was leaving my ears and my face and body were drenched in sweat, after three minutes! But I made it. I did 14 minutes of exercise and Himself assures me that I am still alive, although he is wondering why I am still lying on the floor when I finished exercising an hour ago.

I may be slightly mad, but I'm looking forward to tomorrow's jaunt with LWR. I feel slimmer already.

POLLYANNA, LEAVE ME ALONE

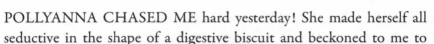

POLLYANNA CHASED ME hard yesterday! She made herself all seductive in the shape of a digestive biscuit and beckoned to me to make a cup of tea and dunk her!

Himself is poorly, and I've tried all manner of tricks to get him to eat, offering soup, fruit, beef stew, etc but no ... he wanted digestive biscuits! So, off I trotted to buy him some. Whilst I was putting the she devil (digestives) in my basket, she began her incessant whispering, as I marched up and down the aisles looking for delicious fruit and wholesome vegetables. I got home, flung her in the cupboard and shouted 'Away demon! Be gone!' But the pesky temptress just laughed, as she knew I would have to see her again when I opened her packet later for Himself.

I found myself grappling with myself and it felt like I had Slimpod (aka Delilah) on one side and Pollyanna (snack habit) digestive on the other. I found that I wasn't hearing Delilah, who was saying, '... but it's just fake food love', and was using willpower! I was flipping distraught, as I hadn't used willpower since I joined this programme. So, I said to myself ... 'Have a digestive if you want one! This is not a diet, so you can eat what you want! Do it!'

I felt absolutely filled with conviction that I didn't want it and had some strawberries instead. Pollyanna fell on the floor in shock, her eyes rounded in horror. She whimpered and moaned and I stepped over her and carried on with my day! Delilah 6,783, Pollyanna 0.

SCALES ARE SO RUDE

I AM ITCHING TO GET on the scales, but I am resisting, because I have begun to notice just how aggressive scales are ... how demanding, bossy and downright rude they really are.

First, they insist on you stepping on them! 'Hurry up, Hurry up, yes take off your earrings that'll make a difference', they sneer. Then they're so flipping rude! 'Yes, you are a great big lump of lardy lard!' 'Of course that chocolate cake you had last night is making your double chin twice as wobbly!' 'No, the salad you had on Wednesday didn't shift anything, because you can't have that much dressing!' 'Yes, stand on tiptoe with one foot on the ground ... that'll work!'

Since making friends with Delilah, I skip into the bathroom and ignore Slimy Simon (aka scales) because he's so judgemental, bad tempered and delivers bad news with smug satisfaction and glee.

Every time I brush my teeth, he shouts at me, 'Have you seen the size of your butt?!' When I use the loo, he says, 'Careful don't break it!' When I smile at myself in the mirror, he shouts 'What ya smiling at moon face!' He is such a sarky slimy sod! So why have I relied on him all these years?! Why do I run to him daily, asking for a cuddle when I know he's going to give me a slap! He is a big ole emotional bully and I'm done with him!

Since I've been ignoring him, he's taken to trying to be nice and says, 'Oooooh, I think your ankles look slimmer. Jump on me and let's see!' When I say no, he glares at me and gets all huffy, but I don't care!

I know Slimy Simon absolutely hates it when I'm happy and wants to steal my joy, so I won't let him and I've banished him to the towel cupboard where he can upset himself. The towels won't stand for his nonsense and will squash him with their Lenor softness if he starts his rubbish!

I have a jiggle in my wiggle and Simon's mad because I no longer feel bad about myself and I no longer measure myself by his standards because I am so much more than that.

SNEAKY ATTACK

YESTERDAY POLLYANNA (aka snack habit) sneaked up on me with an attack from the rear! Usually, she tempts me to have sugary treats, but yesterday she slid into my head and whispered, 'Ya like cashews don't cha?' I was busy reminding myself that scones (full of sugar) are poison, as I had seen a recent luscious example in the store, so I wasn't paying attention. And, really, cashews aren't my binge thing.

I had nuts and seeds in the cupboard, you know ... just sitting there, chilling ... minding their own business and having a nice chat with the soup and the peas, talking about when they might get an outing ... but realising that they weren't the favourites and staring balefully at sweet corn, who smiled sweetly at them secure in the knowledge that she was getting out soon. She knew her little brother, baby corn, got out yesterday, so it was only a matter of time.

Cashew started shoving sweetcorn and shouted, 'Hey ... I'm crunchy and delicious. Come and get me!' Pollyanna said, 'Did you know cashews are good for you too?' My fingers itched, my arms and feet moved of their own volition, and I had stuffed three handfuls of cashews in my face in quick succession, before I could shout, 'Down Pollyanna!' I did actually try to shout at Pollyanna, but my mouth was full. I glared at her and silently promised retribution!

I was bereft and demanded that Himself tell me why I had eaten the cashews! I was slightly mad about the eyes, so he did back away in alarm, but managed to stammer that he didn't know.

I calmed myself and considered whether I might be hungry. I realised I might be, so I ate two bananas whilst I prepared my dinner and smiled happily at the peas.

14 DAYS

WHEW! WHAT A WHIRLWIND journey this last two weeks has been!

I am now more in tune with my body, I know when Pollyanna (aka snack habit) is sneaking up on me and I can give her a hard stare or a slap.

In 14 days, I have had one snack! One! One! One! This is revolutionary! Hang out the flags! I have not binged on sweet or savoury treats for two weeks! I have done this before on a diet, but not without going into battle with myself. There has usually been all out war and skirmishes ...battle-worn, I have emerged victorious, but bloodied from the fights with myself.

BUT, Delilah (aka Slimpod) keeps temptation at bay. There is no fight, and no war. Instead of sugar and crisps, I've thoroughly enjoyed my meals with lots of fruit, veg and the odd seed or nut.

SPACE

SINCE MEETING DELILAH, I have gained so much ... not weight, but Wins! Today, I discovered space in my bra. Himself is less than delighted, but I ran around the room whooping, until I remembered I can't run, as I'm as unfit as a frog, so lay gasping on the floor instead, whilst cupping my reduced breasts and crooning softly, 'Aren't you clever to have shrunk without me noticing? You clever girls!!' I hotfooted it to Poundland and bought three new size D bras, cheap as chips. Well, my breasts may keep shrinking and I'm not able for the likes of Bravissimo or M&S just yet, as I have pronounced that these are the incredible shrinking breasts. D cups, you're marvellous, I love you, you're as cute as a button, fabulous areola and all that, but I'm now aiming for C cups.

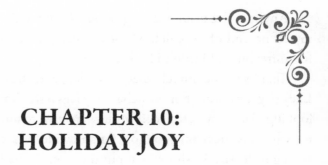

CHAPTER 10:
HOLIDAY JOY

I'm going on holiday soon and, as this was a holiday booked pre COVID pandemic, I'm beyond excited!

I decided to do my packing today, but I wasn't sure what I could pack. In between yo-yo dieting, when I had achieved – yet another – temporary weight loss, I would gaily throw small items into a suitcase in glee, but in the last year, my girth has expanded and no amount of nudging, pushing, shoving, shouting at it, or giving it a slap, would make the weight shift! My belly would stand there laughing at me and say, 'Me and the lads, bingo wings, leg fat and chins have had a chat, and we're giving you notice that, unless you feed us sweet stuff regular and sharpish, we're going on strike and every ounce of fat is gonna quadruple!' Pleading and promises of a large slice of cake next month were met with derisive laughter!

I stood in front of my suitcase looking longingly at my size 16 shorts, when a mad thought assailed me! Why not try them on? I've always loved my legs, but the marshmallow-like consistency that has developed, and the general width and rubbing together, has made me love them a little less. But, hey, I've been doing SP. Pollyanna (aka snack habit) has been subdued, and I recently took my life into my own hands, donned forgiving lycra, and joined Lucy Windum Reed (LWR) in her madness. Well, she calls it exercise, but I call it torture with a smile.

Anyhoo, I've been sweating along with her daily for weeks, causing myself no end of mischief, whilst not being able to breathe. I know I feel different and I think I look different too!

Thanks to the miracle that is Delilah, and the herculean efforts of Lucy to get me out of my armchair, my legs have slimmed down and are looking, dare I say it, toned!!! My legs are now reminiscent of a younger me when my nickname, to those far and wide, was legs!

I got the size 16 shorts out, put them on the bed and stood back to survey them. They looked very small ... they looked very flimsy ... and I wasn't sure that the zip was up for the task I was thinking of giving it. I closed the curtains, lest unsuspecting innocent passers-by got an accidental eyeful of me wrestling with my wobbling belly flesh and had to clutch themselves wailing 'My eyes! My eyes'.

I held the shorts in both hands, flexed my muscles and pulled. Up they went ... higher, higher, almost there. Was that a rip, my hips asked? 'No lads, we're fine', said right thigh. Press on, press on. Zip. Button. Breathe. Woohoo they're on!' The zip is doing sterling work ... the top needs to be long to cover the fact that my lower belly is trying to escape ... but I'm in my shorts! I can breathe ... just. And my thighs are looking sooooo much better than five weeks ago!

In five weeks I've lost four inches off my waist, an inch and a half off each thigh, two inches off my hips and I'm wearing size 16! I can barely breathe, but what's a little breathlessness matter when I'm in my shorts? And breathing is hugely overrated, in any case.

FAMILY DINNER

TODAY I'M GOING OUT to see lots of family for our monthly Sunday dinner! I made some new jewellery for the occasion, as this will detract from any unseemly bulges ... well it won't, but I can kid myself. I had decided on a dress. A little black dress. Well, a pretty big black dress actually ... but the colour may give the illusion of something slimmer. Yep ... miracles ... madness ... kidding myself.

When I last wore this dress, there was no real definition between my waist and my hips and both were rather luxuriously abundant! My hips have always been reminiscent of the front end of a rather nice ship and my waist has always been exceedingly nice, with the shape and thickness of a rather nice Belgian bun ... delightful ... but not always welcome when you're trying to slip into something svelte.

The moment of truth arrived. I put on nice underwear first. I have noticed that a nice matching bra and knickers can lift my spirits marvellously. I closed my eyes and tried to step into the dress. Fell over, banged my shin and decided that was flipping stupid, so I opened them again. I turned away from the mirror, put it on and it seemed to glide past my hips ... so I dared to open my eyes and squinted at myself in the mirror. I didn't dare open my eyes to their full extent lest I was confronted by hippy hip city and vast waist syndrome.

But my oh my oh my! I have a waist! There is definite definition between waist and hip!

My smile is huge! I have begun to change shape! I have lost weight! I am looking mighty fine and I will knock Himself's eyes out when he catches sight of this vision in black. Well, I had better, otherwise I'll need to know the reason why!!

SWEET POISON

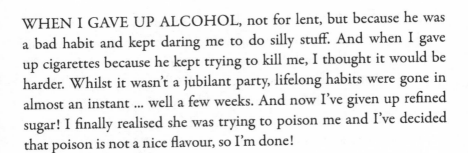

WHEN I GAVE UP ALCOHOL, not for lent, but because he was a bad habit and kept daring me to do silly stuff. And when I gave up cigarettes because he kept trying to kill me, I thought it would be harder. Whilst it wasn't a jubilant party, lifelong habits were gone in almost an instant ... well a few weeks. And now I've given up refined sugar! I finally realised she was trying to poison me and I've decided that poison is not a nice flavour, so I'm done!

ALL MANNER OF NAMES

OVER THE YEARS, I'VE felt shame, angst and viewed my body negatively. I've called her all manner of names, pretending I didn't know her when I went out ... shunning her and starving her ... but now I have fallen in love with her again and I rub my belly every day and say, 'Aren't you deliciously soft and round? I love you so much and I will still love you when you're smaller.'

I want to be smaller ... of course I do. Do I want fewer weeble wobble chins? Yep! Do I want my stomach to enter the room at the same time as the rest of me, instead of entering a few minutes earlier? Yep! Do I want to lose the effect that I have marshmallows secreted about my person in the strangest of places? Yep! Do I want my thighs to stop rubbing together as if in a vain attempt to start a fire? Yep! Of course ... but nonetheless, I am in awe of my body!

SO MANY WINS

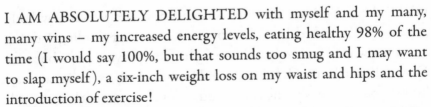

I AM ABSOLUTELY DELIGHTED with myself and my many, many wins – my increased energy levels, eating healthy 98% of the time (I would say 100%, but that sounds too smug and I may want to slap myself), a six-inch weight loss on my waist and hips and the introduction of exercise!

I have discovered that I may be a secret masochist, as I am enjoying the pain! LWR's arm exercise causes me extreme pain, but I love it. I imagine my muscles getting all tight and it makes me smile.

THE BATTLE OF THE BULGE

TODAY, I AM PREPARING to go away for some much needed R&R with Himself, so I prepared to put on my jeans. I approached the task with trepidation because these are my favourite jeans. They used to fit. I used to pull them up in one smooth motion, zip them up in a trice and fasten the button with no exertion. In the last year, I've expanded beyond their capacity, but I still attempt to force them on! Using all my strength to wrestle them past the bang belly and the super-sized hips, I suck in my breath to close the zip, then suck in again for the button. Fat protrudes above the waistline and my lower belly smiles smugly whilst pushing madly against the zip.

I know I've lost inches doing SP, but I was fearful my favourites would let me down, so I armed myself for battle. I applied cocoa butter liberally, so I was well oiled. I collected my accoutrements ... a wire hanger, a shoe horn, etc ... and lay on the floor. One leg, two legs slide on with ease, up over ample hips and only a slight tussle with the button! Hurrah, my old favourites almost fit again!

FAST AWAY

I STARTED THE 16/8 fast the day before yesterday, so perhaps it had me discombobulated for a minute and I am ashamed, as I was a little – well a lot – naughty, and appear to have consumed many, many snacks. But, I have learnt a new word and I am re-framing my evening of all out pigging as an act of *indulgence*. I love this ... it sounds so much better than piggery, n'am for n'am sake, and does not conjure up images of me pushing food into my mouth so quickly that I could barely breathe and resort to snorting through my nose whilst hoovering up the granola mountain.

I HAVE BONES

I LOOK AT MY CHINS daily and rigorously assess whether there is shrinkage in the chinage. Are there fewer acres in the faceage? I examine my stomach hourly to consider whether the rolls are smaller. Do they have the same old bounce and spring, or are they deflating enough for me to tuck and fold them away in my jeans? My thighs are examined carefully. Is there more or less mini marshmallow like texture? Many happy hours are spent groping, cupping and weighing my breasts. Do I look full to bursting, as if I were concealing breast milk, or am I becoming less melon like and moving towards satsuma? These are my daily observations, but I have completely overlooked my collar bones!

There I was, minding my own business and sidling past the mirror in my undies. I often sidle past the mirror, averting my eyes as a full frontal of the carnage that is my stomach can cause me to have a mini melt down when caught unawares.

Anyhoo, mid-sidle, my eyes accidentally alighted upon my left collar bone. I was startled since I had not seen her for at least two years! I pushed up against the mirror contorting my shoulders like a mad contortionist thing and yes! Yes! I couldn't believe my eyes! My collar bone is visible above my flesh!

Himself tried to look delighted when I shouted ... 'I have bones! Look! Look! I have bones!' But he failed miserably, so I have gone back to admiring my bones in the mirror and hunching my shoulders for full effect.

MIRROR, MIRROR ON THE WALL, WHO IS THE SLIMMEST OF THEM ALL?

I WAS TRYING ON CLOTHES earlier this week and trying to determine if I was slimmer or more generously proportioned than last week.

I put on forgiving black but resembled a blood sausage, so tried a brightening green but looked less emerald like and greener about the gills and hips....

I normally use the long wall mirror in the bedroom for these mildly torturous trying on sessions, but I decided to try and see if a piece of sparkling jewellery would liven up the outfit, detract from my tummy, make me lose 28lbs, so turned to my jewellery cabinet to select a piece. My jewellery cabinet has a mirror on it and as I swivelled I noticed that I suddenly appeared more svelte.

I eyed this vision in green and noticed that she was slimmer hipped, waist was nipped in and she was looking mighty fine. I swivelled back to the main mirror and green about the gills and hips was back! I spent a happy fifteen minutes swivelling back and forth between mirrors like a mad swivel thing until I got a bit dizzy and had to sit down....

I knew cameras were dastardly devil's, fashioned from the pit of hell and designed to make us feel yuck and I knew they added 10 pounds but I didn't know that their cousin mirror is just as big a liar!

Anyhoo, I have discovered today that some mirrors tell bigger lies than others and some mirrors are really very friendly and are longing to be your best friend....My jewellery cabinet mirror is now my very good friend and I have called her Sadie. She is absolutely charming, tells me I look fabulous and whilst she might exaggerate just how slim hipped I am that's just what good friends do. Henceforth the rest of the mirrors are dead to me and Sadie is my friend for life.

Himself says Sadie isn't lying and she just has a great perspective....

My advice to everyone is find a good mirror, make a great friend. It just makes sense

CHAPTER 11: TODAY, I CRIED

I started my SP journey six weeks ago and found myself in tears after reading some of the wonderful things written by the fantastic people who started this journey before me. I am not used to introspection and perpetual naval gazing is not my thing, but I realised that I was using food to fix me, whether unresolved grief or some other trauma. But I am delighted that I understand me now ... I know what drives me. That rebelliousness and oppositional behaviour is no longer required as I'm grown!

I have been yo-yo dieting for more than half my life and, today, I felt overwhelmed with sadness because, ultimately, I have been hurting myself with food over and over and over again!

This feels like a breakthrough moment. I feel different today ... I feel stronger, more emotional, grounded. And for some reason, I feel like I can actually do it. I can actually stop poisoning my body with the things that make it ill.

I'm fixed! I'm fixed! Well perhaps not since I am still rather round and still salivate when folk mention chocolate fudge cake.

SLIMY SIMON GOT ME TODAY

———— ⟋⟍⟋ ————

I WAS BUSY BRUSHING my teeth, admiring my collar bones and considering which angle hid one of my chins, when I heard this hissing sound coming from the recesses of the cupboard. I opened the cupboard, extracted a towel and Slimy Simon called out to me. 'Misty', he said, 'I can tell from here that your waist is looking marvellous! And ... oh my, oh my ... have you gone down a bra size? Goodness me, I'm definitely seeing less belly! Why not just jump on ... see what you've lost. I bet you've lost at least half a stone in seven weeks', he said. 'It can't hurt', he said. 'And even if you haven't lost anything, you are feeling so good about yourself, it will be fine'.

I lost my mind for a moment. I forgot how truly sneaky Simon is ... and I jumped on!

I made the momentous discovery that I had lost ... two pounds. The shock almost made me fall off Simon. How the hell was this possible?

I have lost 10 inches, I have uncovered collar bones, I fast for 16hrs a day, I do not snack daily. I mean, seriously – I do not snack. Cakes, crisps, biscuits are no longer inhaled by me ... Ever! Well, I had ice-cream three times, in the interests of full disclosure, but three times in eight weeks! What the chuffing hell!! I enjoy berries for brunch and most dinners are carb free (if you don't count the veg ... and I don't), so what on earth is going on?

I took a few deep breaths – calm yourself woman! Calm yourself! Don't make me slap you. So, to recap, you have lost 10 inches. 'Well, clearly, you haven't!' shouted Pollyanna (aka snack habit). 'You just measured yourself wrong because you are obviously still a fat old lardy-bottomed huge thing. 'Gorgeous, though', she added, since I was looking at her menacingly!

I frantically thumbed through Google, who announced that I could have developed muscle. Well, how the hell could I have done that since I only made scant acquaintance with exercise for a couple of weeks and then left exercise in the dust! 'Perhaps you are retaining water', another article suggested. Well, that's stupid! How can I be retaining water if I'm not drinking any?! Light bulb moment. I appear to have neglected to drink any water for the last four weeks. In my defence, drinking two litres of water was becoming rather difficult, as I was essentially having to wander round with my knickers round my ankles, as I was always on the flipping loo! Sleep had been evading me, and when I clambered over himself for the sixth time in the night, I had to keep shushing him, assuring him that his luck most certainly was not in, and I was just going to use the facilities – again! And no, since I was up already, I was most certainly not going to 'just re-acquaint myself with his nether regions for a moment.'

I can only assume that not drinking water is stopping the weight from dropping off, so I threw Simon in the garden, draped Simba the cat over him and instructed him to do his business. Yes, right there dammit. I drank eight pints of water and I am writing this from the toilet, because unfortunately this is where I live now.

BEACH BABE

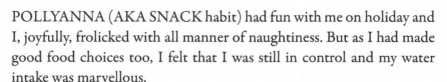

POLLYANNA (AKA SNACK habit) had fun with me on holiday and I, joyfully, frolicked with all manner of naughtiness. But as I had made good food choices too, I felt that I was still in control and my water intake was marvellous.

I was constantly hopping out of the sea and hotfooting it to the beach toilet, but I called it exercise. I made the unwelcome discovery that some people wee in the sea? Ewwwwww, yuck. A complete stranger accosted me on the beach when I was on my third foray from the sea to the loo, and cheerfully recommended it! I tried hard to conceal my horror, but I may have been unsuccessful, since she looked a bit huffy and stomped off in the sand back to her day bed. I told on her to my sisters and we spent the day eyeing her speculatively whenever she went into the sea. I saw her eye us back and then she went to use the beach loo.

On one of my jaunts to the loo, I got chatted up, which was a bit of a phenomenon for me. I have noticed that, as you get older, you sort of become a bit invisible. Well, unless you have your bits out – but that's a young woman's game, which I have put behind me, well most of the time and particularly when my daughter, Iris is looking. Anyway, pretty boy was soooooo young. He asked me, haltingly, if I wanted to go for a drink. I smiled, declined, flashed my engagement ring and immediately texted Himself to tell him that he had competition from men young enough to be our son! He was suitably impressed!

When I got home, I cheerfully went back to intermittent fasting and my berries and yoghurt brunch ... bliss, but I've just realised – by reading someone else's post – that nuts are a feature every day. How on earth did that happen?!

I'm eating about 50g a day and I'm not hungry or thirsty. I just shovel them in like a bit ole shovelling machine!

My name is Misty Brown and I am still a snack addict!

There was me feeling all smug about no longer snacking, just because I wasn't eating all my old favourites ... while I was deep in denial about my nut habit.

Henceforth, nuts in jars are banished and if I fancy a nut, I have to go to the shop and buy a small packet.

I decided that since I'm a big ole addict, I would see what damage my wanton enjoyment had done. And no, I did not jump on slimy Simon (aka scales), as much as he wanted me to – nope, I measured. I have stayed the same as when I measured three weeks ago, except on my hips, where I've lost three inches!!! The water is working!! Yaaay water! You lovely thing you! Water now deserves a name, befitting her queenly status. She is now called Nefertiti.

Nefertiti is fantastic. She often tells me how good she is for me and, when I ignore her, she slaps my legs, shakes her head and tells me how disappointed she is in me. But when I drink her, she tells me I'm a very good girl and beams happily at me. It's lovely to bask in her approval ... and I prefer that to slapped legs, so drink I must.

CHAPTER 12: THE FINAL FURLONG

My first born fruit of my loins recommended that I go for a daily walk, and since Trevor had been banging on about 'moving more' for weeks I decided to take a stroll to my local church this morning, to take in the river and some bracing air.

I was feeling good, listening to gospel music on loud and enjoying the views. In the midst of my smug satisfaction, in rode two dogs running hell-for-leather towards me, with their owner nonchalantly bringing up the rear.

I was so glad that I had been listening to gospel music, and began to pray fervently that these hounds from hell weren't hungry.

A random man, clearing leaves, saw me frozen in fear ... shook his head at me ... and said, 'They're not gonna hurt you.' I was moved to wonder whether he spoke fluent dog, as he appeared supremely confident whilst eying my petrified state with derision.

The owner finally realised that I was terrified because I was shouting, 'Please God no!' – which may have been a clue – and deigned to call them back to him. With a backward look, which I interpreted as longing to sink their teeth into my calves, they bounded off back to him. He said, 'They wouldn't hurt you, love.' Whilst shaking, I explained that since I have been bitten three times by dogs 'acting out of character', according to their owners, I would prefer that he put them back on their leashes. He complied, and I wish that I still drank alcohol, as a leisurely walk – the first I have taken in over 15 years – turned into a terrifying ordeal and I needed rum, intravenously if possible!

I was pretty sure that I wasn't in a dog park and I was also pretty sure that it's not ok to let dogs bound free on pavements. But since he and his dogs don't share my certainty, tomorrow's walk will have to take a different route.

I count a 30-minute walk, and a bonus near death experience, as a Win!

KNOBBLY KNEES

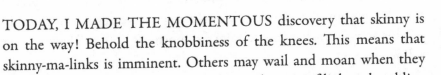

TODAY, I MADE THE MOMENTOUS discovery that skinny is on the way! Behold the knobbiness of the knees. This means that skinny-ma-links is imminent. Others may wail and moan when they sight knobbly knees, but, to me, they are a beacon of light, a heralding of great joy, a missive from on high. The skinniness is almost upon me.

ATHENA, GODDESS OF WAR

SO YESTERDAY, THE REBEL in me got real rebellious! Athena had arrived and was spoiling for war! Sabotage was in the air....

Athena was triggered by someone telling me ice-cream is unhealthy, and giving me a side eye when I said I was going to enjoy a small pot on my cinema date night with Himself. I am a Christian woman, but I was seriously on the verge of channelling Beelzebub, as I was so mad. Pre-baptism, she would have felt my wrath! I could feel myself rebelling, and there was a mighty tug of war going on between new me and my old foe – She Devil Rebel, aka Athena ... crisp-eating, hard-rum-drinking, 20-a-day, Belgian bun-scoffing, biscuit binge-eating, hard-talking, oppositional old rebellious me! New me won, but barely escaped intact, because Athena is pretty damn formidable, rowdy, and direct and will drink anyone under the table. She is also pretty damn seductive, and we used to have so much fun! But she is extremely naughty and I refuse to be *that* naughty again.

The win is that Athena is back in her box. I enjoyed my cinema date night with Himself (Wakanda forever ... absolutely amazing film....I still miss Chadwick Boseman....amazing man!) and my ice-cream, but restrained myself and did not summon Beelzebub for the thoughtless person who tried to food shame me.

I have counted my wins and they are legion. I drink lots of water (aka Nefertiti), I go for a walk almost every day, I eat lovely healthy food, I no longer have an all-consuming daily snack habit (aka Pollyanna), I do not obsess about food or calories, but thoroughly enjoy every meal. I have more energy, I have lost so many inches, I have space in my bra, I discovered collar bones, I have ditched the scales (aka Slimy Simon). I fit into my favourite jeans, I have almost finished writing my first book.... I launched a new jewellery line, developed marvellous knobbly knees, one of my chins is gone and my legs are delighting me again! All in all, I am entering week 12 like a boss!

WICKED WITCH OF THE WEST

I WAS AT MY MARKET stall last weekend, and doing my video reel for Insta, when I caught sight of myself in my display mirror and couldn't believe the length of my chin! I could have given the Wicked Witch of the West a run for her money, if only I had a wart on the end of it. I resigned myself to being less generous with the Greek yogurt and moved on.

However, a miracle occurred today. The chin is still remarkably long but I'm trying to detract from it by wearing red lipstick, as it's one of my gorgeous nephew's birthday and we're off out – en mass – for a celebration dinner.

I reached for my trusty jeans and floaty top, as – after yesterday's witchy chin sighting – I felt sure that I was probably going in the wrong direction in regards waist slimmage, but my hand moved of its own volition and plucked a blue dress from the hanger. I was mighty surprised at the cheekiness of hand, but I assumed that hand was tired and had no idea what she was doing, so I humoured her.

I slipped on the dress and *actually* couldn't believe my eyes. I could see a bit of waist and my stomach wasn't protruding out of the front!

I last wore this dress four years ago and I hoped to fit into it next year ... but, unless my eyes are deceiving me, it fits now!

I reached for the same dress in black, and that fit too, so I went on an absolute frenzy of trying on and throwing off clothes. At one point, I was so excited that I jumped up and down on the bed.

And to round off a fabulous day, Kiki told me that my chin is looking more pointed because my face is slimmer!

THE GREEN-EYED MONSTER

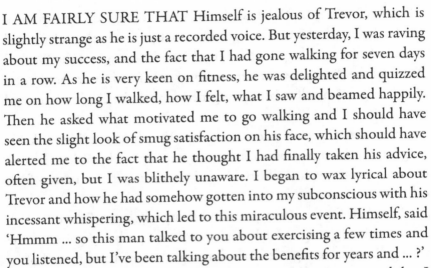

I AM FAIRLY SURE THAT Himself is jealous of Trevor, which is slightly strange as he is just a recorded voice. But yesterday, I was raving about my success, and the fact that I had gone walking for seven days in a row. As he is very keen on fitness, he was delighted and quizzed me on how long I walked, how I felt, what I saw and beamed happily. Then he asked what motivated me to go walking and I should have seen the slight look of smug satisfaction on his face, which should have alerted me to the fact that he thought I had finally taken his advice, often given, but I was blithely unaware. I began to wax lyrical about Trevor and how he had somehow gotten into my subconscious with his incessant whispering, which led to this miraculous event. Himself, said 'Hmmm ... so this man talked to you about exercising a few times and you listened, but I've been talking about the benefits for years and ... ?'

I tried to reassure him that Trevor meant nothing to me, and that I only listened because Trevor made me – that I didn't like him really and actually, on reflection, it probably wasn't Trevor's influence at all and it was just that I finally realised how right Himself was on this matter. He was not appeased and I had to spend the evening saying bad things about Trevor. Sorry Trevor.

I AM NO LONGER INVISIBLE

YESTERDAY WAS FANTASTIC, as I got to sell my jewellery at the Christmas Market, and I pulled. Please don't worry, as Himself is still very much my love, apple of my eye, gorgeousness personified, yada, yada, yada, but I'm delighted that – at the ripe old age of 50, and after a long day selling my jewellery – I've still got it!

Picture the scene ... me tired and hungry. I was so busy, I hadn't eaten all day. My feet and hands were frozen. My lipstick was gone. I had a red nose and windblown cheeks. I really did not feel pretty. Anyway, there I was waiting near a pub for yet another Uber to cancel on me. I was feeling immensely sorry for myself, and may have cried if my tear ducts hadn't frozen in the frosty air. Anyhoo, sounds of revelry were coming from the nearby pub and warm air wafted out every time the door opened. I was suddenly stricken by a desire for peanuts, and I left the jewellery trolley, tables, bags and boxes outside. Frankly, at this point, I wouldn't have cared a jot if they were stolen. I just wanted warmth and peanuts.

I entered and walked purposefully to the bar, but my progress was halted by a large man, who, incidentally, was quite attractive, if you like them beefy and dark haired, with twinkly eyes. He proceeded to tell me I looked beautiful, had amazing hair and asked if he could buy me a drink. I explained that I don't drink, was waiting for my Uber, was engaged (flashed the engagement ring), and was in desperate need of peanuts and warmth. He was very gallant and insisted on buying my peanuts for me. We had a lovely little chat, where he waxed lyrical about my eyes and my hair. Full disclosure – it was a very good hair day, and we discussed the lost art of compliments. He bemoaned the fact that women, nowadays, didn't appear to enjoy a compliment, and I fervently assured him that I thoroughly enjoy compliments, all day, every day. My Uber was approaching, so I wished him adieu and went back out to wait for it. I must confess that I was very smiley, despite the foot numbing cold.

This is the second time I've gotten chatted up in as many months. Yes, I *am* keeping score dammit! Because this is flipping momentous. Whilst I know there have been physical changes, my confidence levels are through the roof! The poor man was obviously helpless in the face of my marvellously elevated confidence levels and sassy walk. Despite the leg warmers, baggy top and bum bag, I was obviously irresistible!

DING DONG, THE WICKED DIET WITCH IS DEAD!

DEAR DIARY,

Today marks the beginning of week 12 and the end of the programme.

I have mixed emotions, because I looked forward to a new coaching video each week with new morsels of greatness to impart.

Overwhelmingly, I feel peaceful because I'm not fighting anymore. Pollyanna is resting and has no spirit left to tempt me. Occasionally, she raises her head, looks over at me and says, 'Awwwww, I can't be bothered ... you're just gonna say no!' Slimy Simon, aka scales, has made his home amongst the towels and has gotten fat and exceedingly heavy.

I have spent a portion of my childhood ... my 20s, 30s, 40s and some of my 50th year battling food. I have sworn at it, cried at it and begged it to leave me alone ... all to no avail.

But now my waist is smaller, my stomach is less duvet and more pillowlike and ... my legs, oh now my legs are looking fantastic again. I've decided that I will insist that people call me 'legs' again, even if they don't want to, and I am happy to slap them about a bit until they are persuaded.

I have found bones again. I mean, I knew that they were lurking under the surface of my skin, but I hadn't seen them for years!

Nefertiti and I are on first name terms, and I no longer have to call her 'Your Royal Highness', since she has agreed that because I partake of her water bounty on a daily basis, I have earned my seat at the royal table. I drink water every day and my knickers are less around my ankles than previously, which means that I can leave the house – on occasion – and go for my daily walk. Me. Walk. I walk every day ... which is a miracle in, and of, itself!

I have boundless energy....

I do not eat crisps ... well, I do ... but hardly ever. I enjoy every morsel that I eat and I feel guilt absolutely never.

I look forward to my vegetables and whilst I haven't gone mad and will never eat a carrot, ewwww yuck ... broccoli and spinach are fast becoming good friends.

I never, ever, ever say I'm being good today, or I'm being naughty today in relation to food. I leave my naughtiness for the proper occasions when harmless mischief is required, or rules need to be broken, or boundaries need to be pushed.

My name is Misty Brown, and I am a 'Normal Eater.'

EPILOGUE

IT'S CHRISTMAS NIGHT and as I wipe away my lipstick, I reflect on basking in the bosom of my family, as I ate, drank, sang and was merry!

I ate a deliciously healthy, smallish ....plate of food, drank alcohol free drinks and didn't freeze my bottom off on the patio as I don't smoke!

I felt beautifully svelte, and my throaty chuckle was heard all day, because I am simply at peace and find joy in everything!

Misty, who are you? Where is that stuffing her face, hard smoking, hard drinking woman gone?

I am dazzling myself with how much I enjoy looking at myself and it is really rather sick making how much I grin at myself in the mirror, but quite simply, I am in love with myself, truly madly, deeply!

ACKNOWLEDGEMENTS

Thank you......

AMANDA FORSYTHE FOR creating the beautiful front cover; you captured Misty's spirit.

PAULA EMERY FOR HER incredible proofreading – best offer I had all year. You are fantastic at what you do!

TO THE SLIMPOD CLUB for encouraging me to do this.... it's your fault!

MY SISTER VALERIE LITCHMORE for listening to me bang on about everything, every single day and for her patience in listening to this plot when I was at my most boring and offering helpful suggestions. For giggling when she read my first draft and for always being my best friend.

MY SISTER KIM LITCHMORE for reading my first draft, writing amazing feedback and for her unstinting encouragement and beautiful words of praise, which I will treasure forever. Thank you for laughing out loud when you read my first draft. It was the moment I really believed I could do this.

MY SON JORDAN LITCHMORE-Lake for always being so appreciative of everything. His integrity, sensitivity, humble and loving spirit always encompass everything that he does. For being such an amazing young man and for bringing me nothing but joy since he was born.

MY DAUGHTER TIA LITCHMORE-Copeland for making every birthday and Mother's Day a wonderful extravaganza, for being the definition of love, for your marvellous moral compass and for your kind and loving heart. She inspires me with her can do attitude to everything, She is my mini me with all the good and none of the bad!

MY OLDEST SISTER CAROLE – the keeper of all the intelligence – thank you for always allowing us to use your brain! My role model extraordinaire! Thank you for being mum to the little ones when we lost our mummy and you still needed your mum. We appreciate you.

MY BROTHER ANDREW FOR your patience, for coping in a sea of sisters, for being so wise and a role model for every black man and for being the best teacher ever! Your students are so lucky!,

MY SIBLINGS DAWN, KAREN and Jonathan for encouraging me.

TO DADDY – MR LISTON Litchmore - For always being our stalwart guide and patriarch, who always kept us on the straight and narrow, providing often infuriatingly spot on advice, when we didn't know we needed it and for teaching us that family is simply everything.

TO OLIVIA – THANK YOU for loving daddy, looking after him and for bringing your stylish and loving self to our family.

MY NIECES AND NEPHEWS who inspire me, are multi-talented, hugely accomplished, for their courage, their love of family and for their unstinting support of aunty through one hair brained scheme after another!

TO MY MUMMY, MRS IRIS Lucinda Litchmore (nee Smith) gone too soon but never forgotten, loyal, loving, playful, wise and so kind. She opened our home to anyone in need, her baking skills were legendary, and she warmed the towels on a rainy day just so we would be warm after splashing in puddles. She was the epitome of love, my inspiration for everything and the reason I am.

TO GOD, WHO HAS KEPT me sane through everything and blessed me so richly. Thank you father God.

COMING SOON!

If you enjoyed this book, please look out for the next book in the series:

The Secret Diary of Misty Brown, Drunk & Disorderly!

About the Author

Denise Litchmore is the author of the novel 'The Secret Diary of Misty Brown', which is a semi-autobiographical work of fiction.

She has two adult children and has a huge extended family, of whom she is immensely proud. She was born in Brixton and has lived most of her life in South-East London, but now lives in Kent and hopes to return to London one day.

Dogs have an unfortunate habit of trying to eat her and her cat left her, as he selfishly created a family of his own, so she vows never to replace him.

In her spare time, she reads, decorates her home, creates beautiful cakes, sews, creates jewellery, which she sells at craft markets, watches lots of American sitcoms, is an avid "Loose woman" fan – and is keen to appear on the show and sit next to Judy or Charlene, because she thinks they would enjoy her....